RICHMOND HOUSE
ASTORIA TRILOGY #1

LEIGH MAYNARD

Richmond House

Copyright © 2022 by Leigh Maynard

All rights reserved.

No part of this book may be reproduced in any form or by any electronic or mechanical means, including information storage and retrieval systems, without written permission from the author, except for the use of brief quotations in a book review.

❀ Created with Vellum

To my husband, who became a reader when I needed him most.

CONTENTS

Prologue	1
1. Greer	7
2. Greer	15
3. Greer	23
4. Greer	31
5. Jace	39
6. Greer	45
7. Jace	51
8. Greer	61
9. Jace	71
10. Greer	77
11. Jace	89
12. Greer	101
13. Jace	111
14. Greer	117
15. Jace	125
16. Greer	137
17. Jace	157
18. Greer	165
19. Jace	171
20. Greer	177
21. Jace	183
22. Greer	191
Author Note	201
Also by Leigh Maynard	203
Acknowledgments	205
About the Author	207

"May God bless you, and may your bones bleach in the sands."

> Capt. H. Lawrence
> Clatsop Spit, Astoria, Oregon
> Oct. 25, 1906

PROLOGUE
GREER

February 2011

I shifted in the semidarkness, uncrossing my legs, and glanced at the clock on the wall above my mother's hospital bed. Moonlight pouring through the thin beige curtains behind me coupled with the ambient light from the nurses' station down the hall made it possible to watch every second pass. Falling asleep was out of the question—the overlapping beeps of the IV pump and heart monitor were muted, but too irregular to form a soothing cadence. The unrelenting odor of bleach burned the back of my throat.

I tucked my hands under my thighs and used my body weight to anchor them in place, the flimsy plastic chair I sat in squealing its disapproval.

Idle hands are the devil's workshop.

I glanced at my mother's face and inhaled sharply at the open eyes that greeted me. Sunken, balanced on a slash of cheekbone that seemed to melt away beneath, her eyes moved over my face.

"Greer," she said on an exhale.

I leaned forward and covered her hand with mine. Hers

was cold and translucent, the small bones as delicate as a baby bird's. I knew I could easily crush them. For a second, I wanted to.

"I'm here, Mother. How are you feeling?"

She stared at me and shook her head slightly, raising her bony shoulders as if to indicate that it didn't matter how she felt.

Only how she looked.

"How?" she asked in a reedy voice. She struggled to swallow.

"You fainted again. I found you on the floor, and when you wouldn't wake up, I called for an ambulance."

She pressed her lips into a thin line.

"I'm sorry," she pushed out through her dry lips. "I don't know why."

Yes, you do. You know exactly why.

"Maybe we should try doing those daily affirmations again. To redirect your focus away from restricting," I said gently, trying to stick to the script her doctor and therapist agreed would be least triggering.

"Haven't been restricting. Not lately." She closed her eyes. Her skeletal fingers moved out from under mine, then slowly through the darkness toward the back of her other hand. She scratched at the side of the tape holding her IV in place in slow motion.

That she hadn't been restricting was a lie, of course. The slender, beautiful woman I remembered from my childhood was now emaciated beyond all pretense of normal. She'd worked toward it every minute of every day, toward becoming so thin, so small, that someday she'd cease to exist. Now, it was the only thing she cared about.

The door to my mother's room opened noisily, and a heavyset nurse in Seahawks-themed scrubs appeared, using her foot to keep the door propped.

"Greer Richmond?" she asked, not bothering to lower her voice even though it was the middle of the night.

"Yes?"

"I need to speak to you. Privately."

My mother's eyes were still closed. The chair creaked again as I stood, the starched white shirt and plaid uniform skirt I'd donned yesterday morning before school now creased from hours of sitting. I smoothed my hands down the front of my skirt before walking past the nurse and out into the hallway.

"Ms. Richmond, I'm Dana. I'll be Blair Richmond's attending nurse for the next twelve hours."

I nodded, suddenly struck by how tired I was. Of everything. The nurse consulted her clipboard.

"It's my understanding that your mother's past diagnoses include anemia, osteoporosis, and acute malnutrition resulting from long-term anorexia nervosa. Is there anything else we should be made aware of? Anything that's developed or worsened since her last hospitalization?"

"Not that I can think of."

My mother was awake when I returned to the room.

"I'm sorry. I was with the nurse." I crossed back to my chair. "She said you're going to have to eat, or the doctor will start pushing calories through the IV. They're going to do it right away, after breakfast if you refuse it."

"Ridiculous," she said on another breathy exhale.

She turned her head to look at me as if expecting the conciliatory nod, the subtle murmur of agreement I'd offered her since she'd first explained to me how misunderstood she was all those years ago. As much as I wanted to give her what she needed, I allowed myself the rebellion of silence. Just this once. When her loaded stare became unbearable, I tapped a comforting pattern against my knee, counting the passing seconds as groups of three, manifesting in my mind with each trio—like a child making a birthday wish before blowing out the candles—that this was our last trip to the hospital. That my mother would be well.

Sensing my mood, she turned away. Long minutes passed before she spoke again.

"I wasn't always this way. I used to not care so much. But my father..."

Speaking cryptically about her father, my grandfather, was something my mother seemed to do more and more of these days. I'd never met Sterling Richmond, even though we lived in Seattle, and he lived just three hours away on the Oregon Coast. When I was a kid, he'd sent letters—one every few months—begging me to visit, alongside birthday cards stuffed with cash and boxes full of presents at Christmas, which my mother promptly returned to him unopened. But I hadn't heard from him in years now. Probably since middle school.

"I was never good enough," she continued. "I was never good enough for him. That house..." She groped the blanket at her side in search of my hand, eventually finding it and executing a weak squeeze I'm sure was meant to convey solidarity. "That house was built on secrets. Lies."

She sighed as if steeling herself against the indignities of the coming days. This wasn't her first trip to the hospital. Knowing she would drift off soon, her body starved for the nutrients it needed to keep her up and running, I floated the question I'd been asking for years in hopes the darkness of night and her ever-increasing willingness to divulge the details of her past would act as a sort of truth serum.

"Who is my father?"

She didn't answer, just locked her jaw and stared ahead, sightless. I pressed on. "Just tell me. Whoever he is, I promise I'll be okay with it."

Her eyes closed again; her raspy breathing evened out. I thought she'd fallen asleep when she began to speak in a hoarse voice so soft it was almost a whisper. "Let it go. Please, Greer. He asked me never to reveal his name in exchange for…"

"In exchange for what? The money he sends every month?"

"The money is just…a means to an end."

"A 'means to an end'? What end?"

"Keeping you away from Richmond House," she murmured. "From the monsters inside."

I

GREER

February 2014

The sun descended slowly, lighting up the sky behind us as we drove from one end of town to the other along Astoria's riverfront highway.

"Are you sure this is the way?" I leaned forward and asked through the cab's open plexiglass window, breathing in the stale remnants of cigarettes past.

A pair of watery blue eyes met mine in the rearview mirror. The identification clipped to the back of the driver's faded maroon seat cover indicated his name was James Ducky. I bet he went by Jim. Probably Jimmy.

Jimmy Ducky.

"Map says it is," he finally offered.

I interlaced my fingers in my lap, holding them together tightly as if praying. Jimmy had a smoker's voice, like tires on gravel, and he seemed to punctuate every few words with a series of hacking coughs. I guess that's why he hadn't bothered saying much on the drive from the airport in Portland. I didn't mind, but the lack of conversation meant I'd sat agonizing over the same repetitive thoughts for the better part of an hour. The closer we got to Richmond House, the more I struggled to control my anxiety. I concentrated on keeping my hands still and looked out the window.

I couldn't stop thinking about the way I'd found my mother's dead body just a few short weeks ago, underneath the ruffled pink comforter of her girlish canopied bed. Her heart had given out after more than two decades spent battling her demons, her body finally deciding it couldn't take anymore.

I felt numb, but not with shock. Her death wasn't a shocking or unexpected outcome. With every passing year—every passing day, really—she'd looked more and more macabre, her eyes hooded, her lipstick waxy on her dry lips, her once-thick, blonde hair wiry and sparse.

Late last year, when it'd become clear she was fighting a battle she wasn't going to win, we'd gone together to preplan her funeral. "Just in case," she'd told herself. So, there'd been little for me to do during the days following her death but wait to lay her to rest.

She hadn't wanted anything to do with the family crypt, but I'd felt compelled to inform Sterling Richmond—her father, my grandfather—of her death and upcoming funeral. While they hadn't spoken since she'd left Richmond House more than twenty years ago, he had a right to know that his daughter had died. As far as I knew, he was her only living relative.

I'd dug my mother's childhood address book out of the box under her bed and found what I was looking for listed under "H." "Home," it read in my mother's hesitant script. "110 Merman Drive, Astoria, Oregon."

I'd written to my grandfather the next day. His reply had been prompt. Succinct. He'd written back that he was sorry for my loss but unable to attend the service. He'd sent a floral arrangement instead—the kind of large, showy piece that dominated the space behind the casket, bursting with enough red and pink roses to supply a small city during Valentine's Day weekend. My mother would have loved it. Her funeral had been a sparse affair—but for one gaudy floral arrangement—with just a handful of mourners at the cemetery on a frosty February morning.

True to his word, Sterling Richmond hadn't attended the service, but by replying to my letter, he'd opened the lines of communication between us again, just as I'd decided to dedicate myself to uncovering my mother's truth. My truth. I'd written him again, asking to visit him at Richmond House. This time, his reply hadn't been prompt. It had taken so long I thought he wasn't going to answer me at all. But he had, inviting me—reluctantly, it seemed—for a "short" visit. At least a few weeks, I hoped.

"Just a few more miles, I think," Jimmy volunteered, managing to keep his cough at bay while executing a turn from the main thoroughfare onto a one-lane road built on a spit extending into the Columbia River. In the distance was a small, heavily forested peninsula.

Now, I was almost there, and for the first time, my mother wasn't around to gate-keep the answers I needed to move on with my life. My return to Richmond House represented the opportunity for closure after a childhood spent struggling to take care of someone I was convinced *wanted* to die. I needed to discover who my mother used to be. Who my father was. Once I did, I could finish college and leave everything and everyone behind once and for all.

I pulled my long hair over my shoulder and started a braid to keep my hands from the endless tapping that had taken over my life the past few years. A "manifestation of anxiety," my mother's therapist had said when I'd asked him about it. Whatever it was, I had put it behind me as well. I didn't need to tap anymore. I looked down at the braid I'd created. It was blonde, the exact shade of my mother's hair, though most of hers had fallen out by the end. Maybe I'd become a brunette. Or a redhead.

New life, new hair.

Jimmy made slow progress up the one-lane road as it rose through the trees, forced to navigate each turn while also making sure no one was approaching from the other direction. My body flashed hot—then cold—with every switchback. By the time the house came into view, I could feel my heartbeat in my ears. The cabbie released an appreciative whistle at the sight of my family's estate.

Just breathe. This was your mother's home. You're going to find out what happened to her here.

On a hill at the center of a clearing stood a magnificent Queen Anne Victorian built facing west toward the mouth of the Columbia River and the Pacific Ocean beyond. The massive, well-manicured lawn I'd seen in the pictures my mother kept in that box beneath her bed had regressed to a sort of unkempt grassy field that surrounded the house. A half dozen or so dry-docked boats in various states of disrepair littered the expanse, broken windows and rusted-out bottoms on display. The foot-high grass took on a yellow hue in the fading light, making it look like they were sailing on a gilded sea.

The road we'd been following faded into nothing at the far edge of the field at least a quarter of a mile from the house. Jimmy looked confused until he saw the well-worn tracks that looped around to his right, approaching from the south. The house looked even more prominent as we drew closer, its regal, forest-green exterior bathed in light.

He pulled to a stop next to two cars parked alongside a modern, detached garage—an impossibly small, red convertible with a soft top that wasn't new but couldn't reasonably be considered vintage, and the same kind of expensive, boxy-looking Mercedes SUV I'd seen pull up to my old high school en masse on visiting days. Were these my grandfather's cars? Or had he assembled a welcoming committee?

I opened the car door and stepped out, my eyes roaming the Victorian's high nooks and crannies, imagining the generations of Richmonds who'd made this house a home, before registering motion in my peripheral vision. Turning my head to the right, I saw a pissed-off Canadian goose galloping toward me at an alarming speed.

"Oh no, no, no," I murmured, grabbing my leather backpack from the floorboard of the backseat, and leaving the relative safety of the interior of the cab behind to jog around the back of the yellow taxi with the bird in full pursuit, wings raised and hissing like the spawn of Satan.

I should've stayed in the car.

While I ran in ever-widening circles trying to outwit the demon bird, or at least render it too tired to chase after me, I looked over to see Jimmy calmly removing my matching set of Louis Vuitton luggage from the trunk.

Unbelievable.

"Garbage!" I heard a woman shout.

Maintaining a safe distance from the goose, I took in the group of strangers standing some ways off—two men and a woman—their twilight shadows lengthening above them onto the house like eerie puppets.

"Garbage!" the woman shouted again. "Get over here, you stupid bird."

The goose gave one last hiss before standing down. At first, I was impressed, but instead of walking toward the woman like a trained pet, "Garbage" strutted around the back of the house to avoid her.

I held up my hand in an awkward greeting as the group approached.

So much for first impressions.

With as much dignity as I could muster, I smoothed my leggings and pushed my white cashmere sweater off my left shoulder before closing the distance between us. We met in front of a wide set of steps that led up to a partial wraparound porch and the house's front entrance. I recognized the beds of crepe-paper blossoms flanking the steps as Evening Primrose, the brand-new blooms bursting open one by one now that the sun was almost down, filling the breeze with their sweet vanilla scent.

I couldn't tell which of the men was Sterling Richmond. Maybe neither was. The taller, fitter of the two wore a lightweight linen suit and a vibe that managed to be both intense and indifferent at the same time. His counterpart, younger and shorter but still in good shape, was sporting a dress shirt tucked into pressed khakis and topped with a blazer. The woman wore her hair in a stylish silver bob, a broad smile pinned to her face. She wore a pink-and-green-patterned Lily Pulitzer sheath that looked out of place next to everyone else's muted tones.

"Greer Richmond," I said, extending my hand to no one in particular, breaking the awkward silence.

"Greer," returned the khaki-wearing man in a booming voice, taking my hand and grinning. "Look at you. You're stunning. I think we've all been rendered speechless."

I smiled and held his gaze for as long as I could, basking in his kindness, letting the warmth seep into my bones.

"Thank you. And you are?"

"Horribly lacking in manners, apparently. Again, I think I might be in shock. When Sterling told us you were coming to visit, I pictured a child, not a beautiful woman. I'm Oren Osborne, a friend of your granddad's here. You can call me Oren, of course."

Oren gestured to his right toward the suited man, the

intertwined double *o*'s on his cufflink glinting in the light. I took my first long look at the man I now knew to be the source of my mother's pain, the root of the insecurity that eventually manifested into the illness that took her life. In his gaze, I could see that he was studying me just as intently. His eyes looked opaque in the dim light, and his lack of greeting made me uncomfortable. I kept my expression neutral and turned back to Oren.

"Anyway, welcome to Richmond House," Oren continued. "I'm sorry about that damn goose. We usually keep an eye out for him, but he hasn't been around the past few weeks. At least not while I've been here. Don't know where he goes, just—poof! He's in the wind. But now he's back. And tonight, of all nights. Strangest thing."

"His name is Garbage?" I asked.

"Garbage the Goose," my grandfather finally took it upon himself to speak, in a voice so clear it was glacial. He tilted his head toward the woman next to him. "Eugenia named him."

"Yes, and this is Eugenia Meade," Oren plowed on awkwardly, clearly tasked with making the introductions. "Eugenia is your granddad's...uh...what *is* your official title, anyway, Gerry? Jack-of-all-trades? Right-hand woman?"

"I've asked you many times to stop calling me 'Gerry,' Oren," Eugenia scolded, smiling at me. "I detest that nickname. It makes me sound like a man."

She held out her hands and took both of mine.

"I'm a *close friend* of your grandfather's. Sterling and I were just heartbroken to hear of your mother's death. If there's anything we can do for you..."

"I'm fine, thanks," I said. As soon as the words were out of my mouth, I remembered Jimmy and the taxi and turned to look for him. He was leaning back against the cab in the driveway, kicking the front tire rhythmically with the heel of his boot.

"Sorry to interrupt," he said, now that he had the group's attention, "but it's time to pay the piper."

"For heaven's sake," I heard Eugenia huff behind me as I walked over to pay the fare. "I told Sterling to arrange a rental car for her so she could drive *herself* from the airport. It would have been less expensive than taking a cab, no doubt about that. Really, she could have driven herself all the way from Seattle. Faster *and* less expensive."

I turned and opened my mouth to tell her I'd never learned how to drive, but at the last second, I decided to keep quiet. I didn't know if it was the years I'd spent keeping my mother's secrets or something about this place, but I was suddenly hesitant to give away any information before I'd had a chance to think it through.

"Come on into the house, dear; dinner is almost ready," she said.

I turned again toward Jimmy, intending to thank him for driving me and to say goodbye, but he was already back in the cab with the motor running. I waved, and he nodded before turning the car in a tight circle and heading back down the tracks toward the edge of the field and the forest beyond.

Well okay, then.

With that, Eugenia linked her arm through mine, and we climbed the old porch steps to the front door of Richmond House, the hollow thud of our footsteps piercing the early-evening stillness bathing the house in calm.

2

GREER

The men followed up the steps, each carrying multiple pieces of my luggage. Eugenia stopped in front of the massive, carved, wooden entry doors. A wide swath of transom windows sparkled above, featuring an intricate pattern of glass that rained color onto the boards at our feet.

"How beautiful. When was the house built?" I floated the question over my shoulder to my grandfather. Eugenia answered instead.

"In 1851. It was the first Victorian built in Astoria. There's one bathroom upstairs that serves four bedrooms—two masters that connect through an inner door, and two bedrooms across the hall, meant for the children of the original owner. They used to connect as well, but that door has been sealed for a long time. You'll see the downstairs rooms on the way to dinner."

"Who was the original owner?"

"A sailor-turned-shipping-magnate named Jonathan Richmond commissioned the house. He was the one who brought your family's shipping business over from England."

"You should give tours, Eugenia," I laughed, genuinely touched at her interest in my family. "You're very knowledgeable."

"Not very, dear. I've just worked here for a long time. You pick up on things, you know?"

Her smile stretched wide as she turned the knob. Once the lock released with an audible *click*, she placed a hand on each door and pushed. Hard. I expected a godawful shriek to split the air, but the quiet shudder was somehow worse. Like a silent scream into the abyss. Like an astronaut lost in space, fully conscious and left to float around until they suffocated. Eugenia worked both doors open to reveal a long, rug-strewn hallway that ran clear to the back of the house.

"These doors are sticky, I know," she said. "We hardly ever use them, but I wanted you to get the full effect of how grand it was to visit Richmond House in its heyday."

"You guys don't usually enter through the front?" I asked, warmed by her passion.

"Oh, no, dear, the back entrance through the kitchen is much more practical. And I'd prefer not to be addressed as, 'you guys.' It's vulgar."

Oren barked out a laugh behind us.

"You're too old-fashioned, Gerry," he said. "She didn't mean anything by it."

"I'm sure she didn't," Eugenia replied, her perma-smile pasted back in place. "As I recall, you never visited Richmond House as a child."

"No, ma'am," I said, determined to make up for my apparently vulgar way of speaking. "We...I never got a chance to visit. But I have seen pictures."

Eugenia again linked her arm through mine and led me across the threshold, past a grand staircase on the right, and down the main corridor. As we walked, Eugenia pointed out the large double parlor on one side of the hall and the office and music room on the other side, the hallway brightly lit in anticipation of our journey. It was evident to me now that the main entrance didn't get much use, though the lingering smells of dust over beeswax and kerosene weren't unpleasant. Unlike the house's exterior, which looked in good repair—especially considering the damaging effects of the salty sea air—the interior showed definite signs of wear, most notably the long hallway rug that stretched from the front entrance to the back of the house. Probably once a bright, blood-red, it had faded to pink in some large, near-threadbare spots. I tried to avoid walking on them as we passed over.

"Well, now that I think about it, I'm sure your mother wouldn't have felt comfortable coming back. Nor would she have been welcome, I think. But you might've been, right, Sterling?" Eugenia asked over her shoulder. "Greer would have been welcome to visit you."

"Of course. She would have been *most* welcome."

I gave a tentative smile, again over my shoulder. It was only the second time since I'd arrived that he'd spoken. That reluctancy I'd picked up on in his invitation? Maybe it was more than that. Maybe he'd hated the thought of me coming, and someone—Eugenia, probably—had convinced him. Either that, or he'd taken one look at me and regretted his decision.

"Did you know my mother?" I asked Eugenia, changing the subject.

"Of course I did, dear. She was an especially beautiful child. Everyone said so."

"Oh, wow. Okay. I didn't know that. How long have you worked here?"

"I came to work at Richmond House in 1969. The 'Summer of Love,' everyone calls it now."

"How old were you?"

"I was fourteen," she said, her hardening tone a warning that I should stop my line of questioning. "And completely alone in the world, much like you."

I'm sure she meant her smile to be comforting, but there was something fixed about it. Something was lurking beneath the surface that I couldn't see, couldn't make sense of.

Eugenia led the four of us into a large dining room with a ceiling that soared above a long wooden table decorated with a table runner and an elaborate floral centerpiece I was pretty sure was fake. An unusual chandelier strung with colored sea glass shone overhead. It was striking, but it didn't sparkle like crystal. The milky light highlighted the water stains that ringed around the table. Four place settings waited at one end.

"Now, dear, why don't you sit here," Eugenia said, pulling out the second chair from the head on the left-hand side. She bustled into the adjoining kitchen as Oren sat beside me, the chair creaking under his weight. My grandfather seated himself at the head, leaving the chair to his right for Eugenia.

"Oren, switch places with Greer," he said suddenly.

Oren had no jovial comeback at the ready. The two men stared at each other briefly, and their unspoken exchange threatened the mood at the table.

"It's okay," I said. "I—"

"Of course," Oren interrupted me, his chair scraping the floor as he stood. I moved woodenly to the chair beside my grandfather while Oren resettled himself on the other side of me. I kept my eyes down and ran my finger over the chipped edge of the plate in front of me again and again. And then once more.

Stop it, Greer!

"Oren," I asked, attempting to keep the peace and stopping myself from indulging in bad habits, "what do you do for work?"

"Ah," he said warmly, the immediate past forgotten much to my relief. "I wondered if I'd get a chance to converse or if Gerry was going to hog you the entire night. Let's see...I make my living keeping the books for businessmen like your granddad here."

"Did you say, 'keeping the books,' or 'cooking the books'?" teased Eugenia, who entered the room with a tray of four salads.

"Keeping the books, of course, my dear," he said, patting my hand. "It's all very much aboveboard. I was also recently elected president of the local historical society."

Eugenia placed a wedge salad in front of each of us with a practiced hand, then went to the sideboard and poured red wine into glasses inlaid with mother of pearl, placing them at the top right of our plates before seating herself across from me at the table.

"Before we begin," said my grandfather, lifting his glass, "I'd like to propose a toast."

Oren and Eugenia picked up their glasses, as did I. I didn't know if they'd forgotten the legal drinking age was twenty-one or just didn't care, but I wasn't saying anything. If anyone needed a glass of wine right now, it was me.

"To Greer. Welcome to Richmond House."

"To Greer," echoed Oren and Eugenia.

I looked my grandfather in the eye before taking a sip of the wine. His eyes were the same light brown as my own, but cold. Watchful.

The rest of the dinner passed in a blur of bawdy stories courtesy of Oren, protests from Eugenia, and my grandfather's silence. By the time Eugenia stepped out to bring us each a dish of ice cream for dessert, my eyes were heavy.

"Greer, if you'd like to excuse yourself, feel free to do so," my grandfather said, startling me.

"I'm sorry, Grandfather. Sterling. I'm not even sure what to call you."

"Sterling is fine."

I nodded, both disappointed and relieved at his unwillingness to embrace familial monikers.

"I think I would like to rest now."

"Of course. You must be very tired after your journey. If you wouldn't mind joining me for breakfast, there are a few things I'd like to discuss with you. Seven thirty sharp. Eugenia!"

Eugenia reappeared, holding two small crystal dishes.

"Greer is going to bed. Will you show her to her room?"

She set the ice cream on the table, and I politely bid my grandfather—Sterling—and Oren goodnight. Relieved it was Eugenia and not Sterling who was escorting me, I resolved to set my first impression of the man aside and begin feeling him out tomorrow at breakfast, forging a connection I hoped would eventually lead to information about my mother. I followed Eugenia back down the hallway to the foot of the stairs where my luggage and backpack were waiting. We each took two bags in hand—my entire life in four suitcases—and began to climb the stairs leading to the second floor. On the wall to my left hung at least a dozen portraits. I studied each as we made our way up. All were oil paintings in gold gilt frames. All were men, presumably Richmonds long dead.

"Sterling thought you might like to stay in your mother's old room. Is that all right, dear?" Eugenia asked. "He's just across the hall in the master."

"I'd like that," I said, so tired now that I didn't care

where I slept. In the upstairs hallway, she opened a door revealing a large, feminine bedroom with what I was sure would be a spectacular view from the front of the house in the morning. It was dark in the room—a single flame flickered in an oil lamp on the table. I wondered who had lit it. Had it been burning all night?

"I wanted to redo the room when I heard you were coming, but Sterling wouldn't hear of it," she trilled. "He's kept this room exactly as your mother left it. And of course, the last time she redecorated was around—"

"Her fifteenth birthday," I said. "She told me."

"Of course," she said brightly. "She would have told you all about her room. She barely took anything with her when she left. I'll leave you now. I'm afraid there's no electricity in the bedrooms. There's a fireplace, but the weather's supposed to be nice next week, so you shouldn't need to use it. There's also the lamp there, and a washstand with a sink and full water pitcher. There's no shower in the house, but when you decide to bathe, the main bathroom is down the hall and has a working plug-in for styling tools and whatnot."

"Got it. Thanks. For everything."

Eugenia paused at the doorway, looking as if she wanted to say something else. In the end, she flashed me her signature megawatt smile and then walked out, closing the door gently behind her.

Waiting for her footsteps to disappear down the hallway, I stared into the gilt mirror leaning against the wall on top of my mother's dresser. I thought of my mother glancing into the mirror as she brushed her hair or put on her lipstick. In the near-darkness, it was easy to imagine her reflection—a little too easy—and for a brief second, I saw her face appear in the glass, her normal face from before she became a walking skeleton. Her chin rested against the crook of my neck like she was coming up behind me for a quick hug. Just as quickly, the image of her face was replaced by the death mask she'd worn when I'd found her in her bed. I closed my eyes and listened to my pounding heart.

Get a grip, G. Now's not the time to imagine your dead mother's ghost.

Turning away from the mirror, I turned the skeleton key that sat in the lock. Too tired to unpack or try to make sense of the flight from Seattle, the drive with Jimmy the cabbie, the murderous goose, the awkward introductions, the strange, forced dinner where my grandfather's lady friend was both guest and server, or the idea that the ghost of my mother was haunting my new bedroom, I changed into my softest T-shirt, brushed my teeth in the sink, and pulled back the pink, ditsy floral Laura Ashley bedspread.

My mother was dead. I'd live here for the next few weeks and try finishing my junior year of college remotely. I thought of my grandfather's toast.

"Welcome to Richmond House," I said out loud, bitterly.

With that unsettling thought in mind, aided by the wine, I pulled the covers over my head and slept.

3
GREER

"Does Eugenia live here?" I asked Sterling over breakfast the next morning. We sat facing each other at a table for two tucked away in a window nook in the same dining room we'd eaten in last night, though no trace of that meal remained. Frozen sunlight poured through the bay windows, highlighting the dust motes that seemed to swirl through every room in the house.

A modest buffet of breakfast fare—fruit, yogurt, granola, and pastries—had been set out on the larger table, alongside coffee in a chinoiserie pot. I'd been almost afraid to pick it up; it'd looked too delicate. The coffee had been hot, but Eugenia was nowhere in sight. I'd shoveled a scoop of granola into some yogurt and helped myself to a banana and two pastries.

"No," he replied, perusing his copy of the *New York Times*. He'd finished reading Astoria's daily paper before I'd come down and had refolded it and placed it next to my plate.

"Is she, like, your servant or something?"

Seconds ticked by.

"She is my *employee*. And a friend of the family."

"What does she do?"

Sterling sighed. "She comes in the morning to lay out breakfast. She also prepares dinner most evenings and sees to the running of the house."

"Does she eat dinner with you?"

"No." He poured himself another cup of coffee from the pot I'd left on the table. "But I invited both her and Oren to dinner last night to meet you. They're the only other people who live on the peninsula."

"Are they nearby?" I sipped my cream-and-sugar-laden coffee in between bites of my breakfast and waited for him to continue. Eugenia had set the table for two, and he'd mentioned breakfast last night, so I was sure he'd expected me to join him, but if he was used to taking his meals alone, I didn't want to seem too pushy. Not when I was a guest in pursuit of delicate information.

"Eugenia lives with her daughter in an outbuilding you would have passed on your way here, and Oren's house is even more remote. And gaudy as hell."

The side of his lips quirked up in amusement. After the chilling first impression he'd made last night, I was relieved we were having a somewhat normal conversation. Somewhat.

"So, is there no cell phone service in the house?" I said, trying for a subtle shift in topic. When I'd woken up this morning, I'd unearthed my cell phone from the side pocket of my backpack only to discover I had no bars.

"I'm afraid not. There's a landline down in the parlor if you need to make a call." He steepled his fingers against his stern mouth. "That reminds me—you haven't mentioned how long you were planning to stay. I'm afraid there isn't a university in town."

"Oh, don't worry about that," I said. "I checked, and it

turns out I'll be able to complete my spring quarter coursework remotely. I just have to choose a historical research project to work on and finish it before the end of June."

"And your senior year?"

"I haven't really thought about it yet."

It was clear Sterling in no way wanted me to settle into Richmond House long-term. The money in my mother's account and savings more than covered this quarter's tuition and living expenses, but I wasn't sure how long my father—whoever he was—would continue making deposits once he found out that my mother was gone. *If* he found out. Without his support, I'd have to take out a loan to cover my final year's tuition. That, or sell my mother's downtown apartment—but I wasn't ready. It's too bad asking my grandfather for help wasn't an option, but I wasn't here for money. Part of me felt like I'd let my mother down by contacting Sterling—the man she'd fought so hard to keep me away from—just days after she'd died. But a bigger part of me wanted answers. She could've given them to me, but she'd chosen not to. At least that's how I justified my actions.

"Just let Eugenia know what your plans are when you know. Do you need anything? Clothes, or..."

An actual standing shower.

"No, I think I have everything I need. My mother...she bought me a lot of clothes. I have more than I need from back home."

"Of course."

I took a moment to look him over. Now Sterling was *my* only living relative. My mother loved me, but she'd been ill, and her illness consumed her every waking hour. We hadn't gone out to eat, hadn't socialized, and she'd spent most of the past few years in and out of various hospitals and rehabs. After years of being on my own, the idea of belonging to a family was intoxicating. It was *almost* enough to cement my loyalty—to my grandfather and the family name—firmly into place, despite the real reason I'd wanted to come to Richmond House. Almost.

"May I ask you a question? You don't have to answer if it makes you feel uncomfortable," Sterling pulled me from my thoughts.

"Go ahead."

"What did your mother tell you about me? About our... relationship...when she was growing up?"

"Nothing really. She said she got pregnant with me when she was seventeen."

"Do you know who your father is?"

"No. She never told me. Do you know?" I felt the throb of my heart in my ears and resisted the urge to cross my arms over my chest. If he did know and was willing to tell me, I wasn't sure I was ready. It's what I came here for and yet I wasn't sure I wanted to hear such life-changing news over a breakfast table on a random Monday morning.

"Unfortunately, no. She refused to tell me at the time and as you know, we've had no contact since the day she left." His eyes flashed, and he clenched his jaw. For a moment, I could sense his anger at my mother, but there was something else there as well. Betrayal.

I took a bite of my second pastry, chewing it three times before swallowing.

"I'm sorry about all the stuff we sent back over the years. I'm sure you went to a lot of trouble and—"

"That was Eugenia. Like I said, be sure to let her know if there's anything we can do to make your visit more comfortable," he continued, smoothly blanketing his previous emotion under a cool veneer of civility. "Once upon a time, I knew how to take care of a child, but those days are behind me. And you're not a child anymore, are you?"

He dipped his eyes to the pastry I was eating and then back to my face, leveling me with a disapproving gaze. The bite I'd been chewing turned to stone in my mouth. He stood to leave, walking in the direction of his study.

"Grandfather...Sterling, I mean."

He turned, waiting. I set the pastry back on my plate.

"What exactly do you expect me to do today?"

"Whatever you want," he said. "Rest."

He turned to leave again but stopped short.

"I forgot to discuss house rules," he said. "There are only three. Always knock when the door to my study is closed, and while you're welcome to explore the other rooms of the house, I insist you stay off the third-floor staircase and out of the attic. The wood is rotting, and it's dangerous up there. And finally, I expect you to be appropriately attired at all times while you're in the common areas of the house. That includes footwear."

After I finished eating, contemplating what exactly it meant to be "properly attired," I wandered back up to my second-floor bedroom, running my hand over the carved newel post at the top of the staircase and admiring the elaborate crown molding that circled the floors and ceilings. In the daylight, the house felt less like a cave and more like an abandoned antique store. Looking down the length of the hall, I saw the set of spiral stairs that led from the butler's pantry off the dining room on the first floor to the second floor and then up to the third-floor attic space. I hoped it wasn't the floorboards that were rotten up there. I imagined pieces of termite-choked wood crashing down on me as I slept in my mother's bed.

I decided to stay dressed in the white jeans and pale-pink cardigan I'd buttoned over my bra earlier in expectation of a less formal breakfast. I sat down on the window seat in my bedroom and carefully unlatched the window. There was no screen, but the rush of fresh, salty air that poured through the crack was worth the danger. I watched the ships traveling down the Columbia River, its navy blue waters so wide it was difficult to differentiate them from the Pacific Ocean in the distance. I could just see the river's mouth, the location of many a shipwreck as captains past and present struggled to negotiate its tumultuous shallows.

My eyes moved over the lawn-slash-field swaddling the front of the house, and I saw a man painting one of the smaller vessels. It rested on top of at least a dozen sawhorses almost directly beneath my window.

I could only see the back of his head and broad shoulders as he moved the paintbrush back and forth with precision, but he looked young. At least, younger than anyone else I'd met here so far. His straight hair was black and shiny, cut long enough in the back to cover his neck. Even though the calendar had just today switched over from February to March in the Pacific Northwest, his tanned skin seemed to glow—like a new penny—under his gray T-shirt. The bold, black lines of a tattoo peeked out from beneath his right sleeve.

As if he felt me watching him, he turned and looked up. His eyes were on mine before it even occurred to me to turn away from the window. And I was frozen to the spot.

He was beautiful. The angles of his face—slashing nose, cut jaw, and high cheekbones—made his broad chest seem almost brutish beneath his fine-boned features. From a distance, his pupils and irises were indistinguishably black, as black as the too-long hair that flopped boyishly over his forehead. He cocked his head to the side and smirked, but I held his stare until it threatened to bore a hole right through me, until I couldn't anymore, unable to bear the intensity.

Now embarrassed that he'd caught me spying on him, I got up and grabbed the paperback I'd been reading, settling into a chair across the room from the window. Questions swirled through my mind. Who was that man? Sterling hadn't mentioned him this morning; why was he here? Did he live here too? His smile hadn't been genuine. He was mocking me. Why would he bother being rude to someone he'd never even met?

I spent the next few hours pretending to read when all I wanted to do was sneak over to the window and see if the mystery man was still painting the boat. I finally slammed the book closed. Part of me wanted to stay in my room all day and take the possibility of interacting with him or anyone else off the table. But another part of me was tired of waiting for the other shoe to drop, tired of not getting what I wanted out of life. And what I wanted right now was to talk to that man.

4

GREER

I found the back door Eugenia had mentioned last night hidden in the butler's pantry. Remembering Garbage the Demon Goose, I tried avoiding another run-in, walking slowly and circuitously through the field, eventually making my way to the front of the house.

Spring had come early to the Oregon Coast. While the air was cold and slightly damp due to the house's proximity to the river, the sky was clear, and the grass was dry. When I finally made my way around to the boat I'd seen from my window, the mystery man was nowhere in sight. A long, green garden hose spilled out of the back, and I absentmindedly picked up the end and started coiling it.

One loop, two loops, three loops, pause.
One loop, two loops, three loops, pause.

There was nothing wrong with the number three or counting to three to calm down in a crisis or coiling a hose three loops at a time—I just had to remember that there was nothing magical about it either. There was nothing about the number three that offered protection.

Isn't that obvious now? It didn't save her.

Eventually meeting resistance, I yanked the hose as

hard as I could, attempting to dislodge it from whatever it was caught on so I could resume my count. A loud yelp split the air, startling me, and I watched the vessel shudder, worsening its already precarious position on the sawhorses. I dropped my careful coils and ran around to the front, but I didn't see anything. Then I heard a voice above me, coming from inside the boat.

"A little help?" The voice was deep and tinged dark with anger.

"Oh my God! Yes! Just give me a second."

I ran back and boarded quickly, hoisting myself up a stepladder near the propeller and hoping the boat's perch on the sawhorses had stabilized. I tried avoiding the interior spaces I could tell were freshly painted by the smell that hung in the air. Toward the bow, I found the man I'd been watching from my window flat on his back, his right foot caught in the hose I'd pulled out from under him. Everything above his waist—neck, arms, hands, and chest over and under his shirt—was covered in globs of thick paint, the white a jarring contrast to his bronzed skin. I spotted the overturned paint can nestled in his left armpit; the brush was still in his hand. Even the cheap headphones he'd pulled out of his ears after landing on his back were dripping paint from the cord.

I stood, stunned, taking everything in, trying to make sense of what had happened. We eyed each other warily.

"You must have really needed that hose," he said evenly.

"I'm so, *so* sorry. I didn't think..."

He used his abs to pull himself halfway to sitting. When I didn't automatically move to help him, he held the brush out to me.

"Take this," he commanded.

I obeyed, grabbing the brush from his hand, trying not

to get paint all over myself. He was finally able to stand. I tried unsuccessfully not to stare.

He'd looked imposing from the window, and I was sure standing on the upturned bow gave him extra leverage, but he was tall. Very tall. So tall that if I walked up to him, the entire top of my head could fit underneath his granite jaw. I was taller than average myself at five feet eight, and I'd never seen anyone so physically imposing. Definitely not any of the boys I'd gone out with over the years.

And that was before he took off his shirt.

It was up and over his head in a matter of seconds, revealing his big chest, ridiculous muscles, and acres of smooth skin. His defined core drew my eyes, but it was his arms that held my attention as he began using his ruined shirt to swipe the wet paint from his body onto the deck. Every muscle from his deltoids to his long fingers was perfectly defined. I wanted to laugh uncontrollably at how perfect he was, my emotions teetering between admiration and cynicism. The tattoo I'd seen earlier depicted a geometric rendering of towering evergreens against a jagged mountain range. There was another, on his left bicep, depicting a simple, traditional-looking anchor.

I continued to stand there open-mouthed, watching him while he did his best to clean himself up.

"So, whatever school you go to must be all girls then," he bit out, snapping me out of my full-on perusal of his body.

"I'm sorry," I repeated. I searched my brain for something appropriate to say. Something conversational. "I like your tattoos."

"Hand me those rags." He didn't acknowledge the compliment, gesturing to a pile of ratty towels behind me.

Rude, rude, rude.

I threw them at him one by one, and he sopped up the

excess paint on the deck. Of course, the entire front end would need a good scraping and probably a complete paint job now instead of just the areas he was touching up, but at least there were no open puddles of wet paint anymore.

He moved to the back of the boat, stuffing his shirt and the towels into a plastic grocery store bag he'd had on deck. I followed, handing him the paintbrush, which he added to the bag before neatly tying it off. He took a seat, his legs dangling off the edge. When I did the same, he scrubbed both of his hands down his face.

"I just wanted to say again that I'm sor—"

"You don't have to keep apologizing for finding me attractive."

"I wasn't apologizing for that," I sputtered out.

"No? For what then?"

"You know why. For pulling the hose out from under you and knocking you down."

"I'm just surprised you're apologizing at all. In my experience, Richmonds don't apologize for shit."

"How do you know I'm a Richmond?"

"Are you kidding?" He did his best impression of Sterling but ended up sounding more like Jafar from the Disney movie *Aladdin*. "'My granddaughter, Greer Richmond, is coming to visit. Please make sure you're appropriately attired at all times and avoid interacting with her.' Uh-oh. Zero for two."

I laughed. That definitely sounded like my grandfather. His high-handedness annoyed me. "You're serious? He told you to stay away from me?"

"Serious as a heart attack."

I winced slightly at his words but pushed thoughts of my mother away.

"How long are you going to be here?" he asked.

. . .

"You mean on the boat, or here—"

"I mean here. At the house. With Sterling."

"You ask a lot of questions for someone whose name I don't even know." I went for light and flirtatious, but it fell flat. His eyes narrowed in annoyance.

"Look, *sweetheart*, I don't give a good goddamn. I was just trying to make polite conversation since you insisted on sitting down next to me. I'm heading out now. See you around."

He scooted back, preparing to stand up again.

"Okay, fine, I'll tell you," I said, not wanting the conversation to end, not ready to return to my bedroom. I scissored my legs back and forth below me. "At least a few weeks. Maybe longer. My mother died last month."

He didn't react. I'd just dropped what I thought was a bombshell, and he was giving me...nothing. Not even the canned "I'm sorry for your loss" I'd heard so many times before. Not even a "What happened?" Finally, he spoke.

"So, you were sent here. Is Sterling, like, your guardian now or something?"

"What? No. I don't...I don't need a guardian. No one sent me here. I'm an adult. I turn twenty-one in a few weeks. I'm a junior at the University of Washington. In Seattle."

He raised his silky eyebrows, feigning fascination.

"I must be missing something then," he said. "Your mother died, and you left college to spend time with your bereaved grandpa?"

"Not exactly. I—"

He smirked. "I can't believe you straight-up left college to come on some sort of perma-vacay at this creaky bag of bones."

My temper flared. "Who are *you*? Why are *you* here?"

"Me? I'm Jace Blackwell. I work for Sterling. Isn't that obvious?"

"Not really. Are you in school?"

"Nah. Dropped out my senior year—of high school."

"And how many years ago was that?"

"Woah. Now look who's trolling for information..." His liquid black eyes shifted upward as he did the math in his head. "Eight, I think."

That would make him older than I am. Several years older.

"Why did you drop out?"

His lips pressed into a thin line, as if he was holding back words threatening to spill from his mouth. Either he was keeping himself from telling me or he was keeping himself from telling me off. After a few seconds of silence, it became clear he wasn't going to answer.

"Sorry. Was that too personal?"

"It's fine," he said, his expression guarded. "But I really do need to get going now."

"Just one more question—what's with the boat graveyard?"

He stared at me a moment, piercing me with his intense gaze before throwing his head back and barking out a laugh.

"'The boat graveyard.' That's great."

"So, what's it about?"

"I'm surprised Sterling didn't tell you. He loves old boats. I do too. He's been collecting them for years. I guess he used to fix them up and sell them off, like as a hobby or something, but he's too old now. He hired me to spend a few hours on them every morning."

"So, he's planning to sell them? Once you're finished?"

Instead of answering, he checked his watch before he jumped off the back of the boat and—reluctantly, it seemed

—extended his hand to help me down. His palm felt warm and dry. I tried to think of something witty to say, but before I could say anything, he walked off with the bag toward an old, blue Ford Bronco parked at the bottom of the field.

5
JACE

The lyrics to the song "Closing Time" rang in my head as I swung my large frame into the cab of my Bronco. Except I *did* have to go home. I was late to give Jesse his pills.

Hopefully, the rest of the paint on my body was dry enough not to mess up my car, dry enough to flake off and keep the old man's questions at bay. The last thing I needed was for him to find out I had a job that paid good money. He thought I went to the library every morning.

What a way to meet the girl.

She was gorgeous, of course. Most rich girls are, to varying degrees. I learned a long time ago that if you're not careful, their big eyes and perfect curves will go to your head, and you'll start thinking their attention is genuine. Trust me, it's not.

I started up the engine and looked up toward the house, but she'd already disappeared inside.

Did you think she'd be waiting around just to watch you drive off?

Case in point. I rolled down my window and took a deep breath of fir-tree-scented air before I shifted into drive and began the twenty-five-minute slog from Richmond House, Astoria's literal House on the Hill, to the Navy Heights Mobile Home Park. God, I couldn't wait to get out of that trailer park, and Sterling was my ticket. The money he paid me every week to work on the boats was adding up fast, and soon I'd be able to get my own place and really think about what I wanted to do with my life. Maybe go to college myself, though I couldn't stray far. Maybe just community college to start. Greer Richmond's hoity-toity university degree could kiss my ass.

When I'd dropped out of high school, before Jesse decided to try his hand at drinking himself to death, I'd gotten my GED and joined the navy. I'd made good money during my four years at sea, money I'd spent almost as fast as I'd made it. The four years passed quickly, but Jesse's health had been too frail for me to re-up. By the time my superiors had approved my honorable discharge, I had less money than when I'd gone in.

I refused to apply for a loan, though. One, no one in their right mind would give me one. I worked for Sterling under the table, so there was no record of any employment since I left the armed forces. Hell, I didn't even have a bank account. I didn't want one, not with the threat of garnishment for Jesse's debts—medical and otherwise—looming over me. And two, because I didn't ever want to owe anyone anything. Not ever again. I just hoped Jesse recovered enough someday for me to use my GI bill to get a four-year degree from a good school. In the meantime, I needed to get out of the trailer park. It was time.

Again, Greer Richmond's heart-shaped face made its way into my mind. When Sterling warned me off, he'd talked about her like she was a kid or something. Come to find out, she's twenty fucking years old.

I'm glad I didn't know that when I saw her up in the

window. I might have resorted to a few "inappropriate" gestures to kill the attraction I'd seen all over her face. Instead, I'd tried to stare her down, intimidate her, but she'd turned the tables, refusing to break eye contact, and I'd had what felt like an out-of-body experience. It was uncomfortable, like staring directly at the sun, but there was no way I was going to be the first to look away.

I'd spent the rest of the morning wondering how long it would take her to come down from her tower to investigate further. And what a sight she was when she finally appeared. All that icy-blonde hair should have made her look cold and unapproachable, but even flat on my back and covered with paint, her unusual light-brown eyes and skin pinked up like a peach with embarrassment made me feel...warm. Very warm. And that was before I got a good look at her in her tight jeans and sweater.

But I wouldn't be touching her. Ever.

I've dated around plenty if that's what you want to call it—experimented plenty with neighborhood girls and the girls who'd gone to school with me. I'd never had a girlfriend exactly, but there always seemed to be one or two women around town looking for a thrill, willing to do whatever I wanted. And what I wanted to do with Greer the first time I saw her? I literally couldn't afford to take the risk. Not when I was so close to starting over.

For that reason alone, I was going to stay far away from her, no matter how thick her hair was, no matter how good she smelled, no matter how perfectly polished her toes were. She thought I was hot. I could tell by her shocked expression in the window and by the way she stared at me when I took my shirt off on the boat, but she didn't realize my looks were just an illusion. A byproduct of my beautiful Native American mother and Jesse, my once-handsome, piece-of-shit, white-trash father. An accident of birth. If my looks mirrored where I came from or who I was on the inside, she wouldn't have bothered with me. I was not saying she's a bitch or a snob or anything—I didn't even know her. It's just the way things worked around here.

A fling was all I could ever hope for with Greer Richmond. A fling that could easily get me fired. She had a plan for her future, and I doubt it involved a trashy half-breed. What she didn't know was that I had plans too. Lots of them. And they did not include her or any of the other thirsty women in this town.

I pulled onto the cracked slab of pavement next to the trailer I shared with my old man just in time to watch him open the door and try to walk the three steps down into the weed-filled yard without falling over. I looked at my watch. 12:32.

"You're late, son! Where've you been?" he hollered at me once I opened the door to get out.

"Just lots of traffic today," I said. "Have you taken your meds?"

"Was waitin' on you—but you have better things to do, right? Where'd you say you'd gone off to? The library? Is that, like, code for gettin' your dick sucked?"

He cackled until his face turned red, then collapsed into one of the two cracked plastic lawn chairs set amongst the weeds.

"Yep. The library. Just reading and lost track of time."

"Reading," he scoffed. "Always was the smartest son-of-a-bitch on the block. Never understood how someone so smart could be so damn dumb at the same time."

I jogged inside to mete out the medication and grab the oxygen tank that kept him alive. He wouldn't take his medications unless he got them from me, didn't take care of himself at all. It was his way of keeping me there with him so he wouldn't have to be alone. And it worked. But it wouldn't work for much longer. As soon as I could afford the daily visits from a nurse, I was out.

I came back outside to find his face even redder than before. I practically shoved the cannula into his nose and offered him the pills I was holding in my palm. He took them without water on a practiced swallow.

"Saw your whore mother two days ago at Can Alley," he said, hoping, I was sure, to taunt me into losing my temper. "Didn't actually see her though 'cause I never leave this place thanks to you. But Dave seen her. Said she looked like an ugly, used-up slut and was high as a kite. Good thing she used to be pretty, or you wouldn't even exist."

Thankfully, hearing him talk shit about my mom—once a proud member of the Chinook Indian Nation, who'd abandoned us when I was fifteen—was old hat. I didn't blame her, not really. She'd been a good mom until she'd turned to drugs. She'd started out just wanting a temporary escape from him. Same as me.

"Jesse, I told you I'd take you with me to the store or for a walk or whatever, but I'm not taking you to a bar. You can't afford to start a tab, and it's going to fuck up your meds."

"What's the point of being alive, boy, if all I can do is sit around in this shithole waiting to die? Have you forgotten that I saved your life? You wouldn't even be alive right now if it weren't for me. You owe me. Big time."

I winced. I hated that he had something on me to hold over my head. Jesse *had* saved my life—twice if you believed my mother tried to abort me, which I didn't. When I was a kid, I'd almost drowned in a nearby reservoir pond. Jesse, who'd just happened to be walking by, had—out of the kindness of his heart—stopped to fish his own kid out. And he'd never let me forget it.

I took a seat beside him and looked out toward the

other trailers in the park. We were too far inland to see the river or feel the ever-present breeze that rolled off it in waves. Everything here was stagnant. Used up. Dying. It even smelled like death, like an opossum had been trapped, killed, and was now rotting under one of the trailers.

"What's that on your neck?" my old man slurred, confirming that he'd somehow gotten his hands on a six-pack while I was away. I only hoped there wouldn't be another negative interaction with his medication. Or maybe I hoped there would be. I ran my hand over the back of my neck and felt the thick, scratchy patch of dried paint.

"Nothing. Just leaned against a freshly painted wall while I was downtown."

"Stupid fucker," Jesse murmured under his breath before passing out in the chair, gasping away despite his oxygen flow.

Yeah. Stupid fucker's right.

6
GREER

I woke up this morning to the sound of rain battering the windowpanes in angry, sudden spurts. The long, mild days that hinted at the possibility of an early spring had turned cruel this week. So much for March coming in like a lion and going out like a lamb. More like the other way around. Seattle's blah gray winters sometimes felt endless, but there was a violence here and an unseeable dampness that seeped into every nook and cranny like fog. Like mold. I swore I felt it in my bones.

Equally depressing was the fact that Jace Blackwell has gone out of his way to ignore me since the morning we met on the deck of that boat two weeks ago. He still came to the house almost every weekday, working on engines and whatever else he could manage underneath the portable canopy Sterling had set up to keep the rain out—but he hadn't acknowledged me.

The first few days after Jace and I met, I'd occupied myself by thinking up ways to pass by him while he was working in the field—pretending Eugenia wanted me to pick the raspberries that grew at the edge of the woods, pretending to explore the grounds, pretending that exercise was of the utmost importance to me. Every time I passed him, I'd smile and wave, but he'd ignored me flat. Now I didn't even bother. Besides, there was no way he'd believe I just happened to be taking a walk outside anytime during the past few days. Not in this weather.

It's not like I was trying to pursue a *relationship* with him. We didn't even have to be best friends. But we were here all day together—the only two people for miles under the age of fifty. It was pretty shitty of him to just act like I didn't exist.

Communication with Sterling had dried up within days of my arrival. The first few mornings, he had asked me about my mother, and we talked about what I knew about their falling-out, which was nothing. He never volunteered additional information; he just wanted to know what she'd told me.

After I sat through another breakfast during which I ate next to nothing in complete silence while he read his newspapers, I went back to my room to watch the sheeting rain outside the window and contemplate my next move. I saw Jace pull up to the field just before eight. I kept hoping he'd look up at me and hold my gaze like the first time I saw him, but he was all business as he left the Bronco and walked straight to the rusting old boat that would soon benefit from his attention. He wore his usual jeans, and his head was bare, though today he'd thrown on a worn, navy blue peacoat over his T-shirt in a nod to the rain. It didn't look waterproof, per se, but he was probably used to the icy breeze whipping off the river.

I turned my back on the bay of windows and shook my head. I needed to do something more constructive with my time. I wanted information about my parents and, I'd decided, about what exactly had caused my mother to flee this house and never look back, but these weren't the sorts of thing I could just casually ask Sterling or Eugenia about. The longer I wandered the halls of Richmond House on my own, the more I realized that I was going to need some sort of premise. Here, no doubt, the best course of action was subterfuge. But I didn't even know what I was looking for.

The main staircase at the front of the house deposited me directly in front of Sterling's first-floor office door a few hours later. I knocked on the heavy wood and waited. I just hoped I'd waited long enough to catch him on his lunch break.

"Enter."

He sat behind a massive desk like a king on his throne. Dressed in slacks and a thin, expensive-looking sweater layered over a button-up dress shirt, he resembled no grandfather I'd ever seen. His features were hawk-like, and his body lacked the pleasant roundness of other men his age. He rose to his feet as I crossed the threshold. I immediately noticed the lack of a computer, of electronics of any kind, on his desk. Instead, neat piles of paper covered its vast surface.

"Good day again, Sterling." I thought I saw him glance at the white sneakers on my feet before meeting my eyes. "I'm sorry to come in like this when you're working, but I need a ride into town today, and you did say I should come to you immediately if I needed anything."

He'd been amused when I'd finally confessed last week that I'd never learned to drive, telling me I needed to learn. So far, he hadn't made himself available to teach me. His brows pinched together at my declaration.

"I told you to go to Eugenia."

"Oh. Right. Is she here?"

"May I ask why you need a ride? Do you have an appointment somewhere?"

"Not exactly. But I need to start on my project. For

school. I've decided to research the wreck of the *Jonathan Richmond*."

"The wreck of the *Jonathan Richmond*?" He carefully pronounced each word as if practicing enunciating in a foreign language.

"I assume you're familiar. I got the idea from the model in the parlor."

"She was a beauty," he murmured.

"And I remembered Eugenia mentioning that a Jonathan Richmond commissioned this house. Are they the same man?"

"No. The Jonathan Richmond who christened the ship after himself was our Jonathan Richmond's grandfather. He founded the family shipping business in England in the early nineteenth century and worked to acquire a fleet of ships, the first of which he named after himself."

"Fascinating," I said, laying it on thick. "Anyway, like I said, I'm planning to spend the next few weeks digging into our family history, but I need to check out books and access the Internet. I already have the computer my...mother... bought me for school."

Sterling sat back down in his chair, which was black, sleek, and surprisingly modern, considering the heavy wood and dusty tapestries that made up the rest of his office space.

"The next few weeks digging into our *family history*?"

His dark tone struck me as a warning.

"I mean, at least as it pertains to the shipwreck," I hurriedly tacked on.

"I see. Well, of course, you're welcome to come and go as you please, but I'm occupied for the duration of the afternoon. Oren is quite insistent that I complete this quarterly financial accounting as soon as possible, so I'm afraid I just don't have the time."

"Maybe Eugenia can take me? Or I could ride the bus?"

Sterling scoffed.

"I'm sorry, dear, but the bus doesn't come anywhere close to Richmond House, and I'm unsure what Eugenia is doing today. Perhaps we can—"

"What about Jace?"

"Who?"

"Jace Blackwell? You know, the man who works for you? The one who's working outside right now?"

"Blackwell?" Sterling rubbed his long fingers over his chin. "I see you're already on a first-name basis."

"No. I mean, yes, I guess. I've only spoken to him one time. I just thought that since he's here, it might be an easy solution."

Sterling stared at me, deep in thought, fingers still massaging his jaw as he considered my suggestion.

"You're an adult, Greer, and I can't technically stop you from becoming romantically involved with whomever you wish, but I feel I need to issue a request that your dealings with Blackwell be kept strictly professional. He's an employee, not a social equal. The last thing this family needs is a repeat of your mother's mistakes."

I tried to mask my shock at his words with a nod and a tight smile, trying to process what he'd said as quickly as possible. Yes, I'd attended private school all my life, but I'd never so much as overheard anyone refer to anyone else as a social inferior, much less label them so during a conversation I was taking part in. And repeating my mother's mistakes? Was my father an employee of Sterling's? Or had he been talking about her dating men he considered inferior in general? Or becoming a single mother at a young age? Because the latter wasn't a concern when it came to Jace Blackwell. He could barely stand to be on the same boat with me, much less...

"I understand completely," I said. "My only interest right now is school and a ride to the library. I don't even know the man."

I just know he's hot and I'm bored.

Sterling stood again, turning toward the windows that wreathed the back of his desk. In the distance, I saw Jace working underneath the tarp, head bent in concentration. Sterling tapped the glass sharply. When Jace didn't look up, he unlocked the window and pushed it open.

"Blackwell!" he yelled out over the sound of the downpour.

Jace looked toward the shout, and Sterling gestured for him to come into the house. Shoving the window back down and locking it, Sterling returned to his desk, and we waited. What seemed like such a good idea when it'd popped into my head minutes ago now felt terribly embarrassing. Jace wanted nothing to do with me, and I'd just talked my grandfather, his boss, into forcing him to spend time with me. My fingertips began tapping a pattern of comfort onto the sides of my thighs.

No, Greer, stop. It's fine. It will be fine.

Fortunately, I didn't have much time to contemplate before Jace appeared in the open doorway, his coat slung over one arm, holding his dripping boots.

7
JACE

"Blackwell," Sterling greeted me evenly.

"Mr. Richmond."

I saw Greer standing off to the side of Sterling's desk. She wore a fuzzy, light purple sweater today that reminded me of the scraggly lilac tree at the entrance to the trailer park that bloomed for a week or so every year in the spring. The sweater cut off a few inches above her leggings. My eyes lingered for a beat on the ribbon of exposed skin before moving toward Sterling. He didn't seem to notice me checking out his granddaughter. Or maybe he didn't care anymore.

Unlikely.

"Congratulations, Mr. Blackwell. I've decided to expand the scope of your work here at Richmond House." He glanced at my socks with obvious disapproval.

I stayed quiet, shifting my weight from one foot to the other, still holding the tops of my boots in my left hand. Everyone knew Sterling hated when people took their shoes off—or worse, walked around barefoot. The guy hated feet. But I didn't have a choice; my boots were soaked, and I didn't want to leave them alone on the back porch because they were my only pair. I knew logically that no one was going to steal my boots off the back porch of Richmond House, but I still couldn't take the risk. The office reeked of furniture polish and mothballs, and it was giving me a headache. I wasn't sure where he was going with this, whether the news was good or bad. But Sterling coming off like an elitist dick was something you could set your watch to.

"This is my granddaughter, Greer Richmond. She told me you've already met."

I looked at her again and watched her cheeks turn pink. She wouldn't meet my eyes.

What exactly are you up to, sweetheart?

"Yes, sir. Once before."

I thought about mentioning to Sterling that it was Greer who was responsible for the catastrophe a few weeks ago that had cost him hundreds of dollars in paint and me an entire week's worth of work, but I didn't. She deserved all the blame, but Sterling had been fair about it, and I didn't want to be responsible for her getting in trouble. I don't know why I cared, but I did.

"Ms. Richmond, unfortunately, has yet to learn how to drive," Sterling continued. I grinned ear-to-ear—couldn't be helped. Greer was twenty, and she didn't know how to drive? That was some funny shit. I glanced in her direction and thought I saw her roll her eyes. "I need you to take her into town today and wait with the car until she's ready to come back."

Fuck. No.

Was this her idea? She'd been trying to get my attention the last couple of weeks, and while it was getting harder and harder to ignore her cute little schemes, the fact remained that getting involved with her—in any capacity

—wasn't a good idea. I already thought about her more than I should.

"Sir, with all due respect, the work you want done on the one yacht alone is taking—"

"My granddaughter's needs take priority over vessel repairs, and right now, she needs a driver. Are you willing to support the needs of this family, or shall I find someone else?"

I squared my shoulders and stood as straight as I could in my stocking feet. I glared at Sterling, still seated behind his ridiculously large desk, in a way that made it clear I didn't appreciate the question. Yeah, he paid me well and under the table, but I'd done literally everything he'd asked me to do and more for years now. How dare he question my loyalty and threaten to hire someone else? I opened my mouth to tell him so, but Greer interrupted me.

"Please, Jace. Mr. Blackwell, I mean. It would only be temporary," she said in a smooth, practiced voice, her big, honey-colored eyes imploring me to calm down.

Now all I wanted to do was rattle *her* cage. It wasn't fair that I was losing my shit over here, and she seemed so unaffected. Not when I suspected she was the cause of all of this. I gazed at her intently, slowly tracing her shape from her ankles to the slight flare of hips, all the way up to her full chest and lips. I wanted her to feel my gaze like it was the tip of a flame —heat mixed with pain. My cock throbbed to life in my jeans.

She took a shaky breath and stumbled on.

Not so calm now, are you, sweetheart?

"My...Sterling promised me lessons, and I'll be driving myself in no time. You wouldn't even have to use your car. And you wouldn't have to wait around—you could do anything you wanted while I'm...occupied. Easiest job you'll ever have."

"I'm sure you would be," I insinuated.

"Greer, please," Sterling interjected. "You needn't beg. You're embarrassing yourself—and me. Either he's willing to do whatever needs to be done, or he isn't."

She pasted a bright smile on her face, but I could see Sterling's comment had stung. She was so easy to read. Every emotion she had flitted across her face like she didn't understand how to hide them away. Either that or she'd done it for so long that she couldn't anymore. I felt a pull in my chest, and I knew I was about to do something stupid.

Without turning away from her, I gave my answer.

"Of course, Sterling. You know I'm willing to do whatever needs to be done."

"Excellent. I trust you'll keep in mind everything we spoke of prior to Ms. Richmond's arrival."

"Yes, sir. I'll keep it top of mind," I said, allowing a slight edge of budding sarcasm to creep into my voice. Then to her I said, "Be ready in an hour. I have tools to put away in the shed out back."

Stomping out of the office without a backward glance, I flung open the back door of the house and paused on the steps to pull my boots and coat back on before heading back out into the rain, sloshing through the muddy yard with no regard for the bottoms of my jeans.

That girl was dangerous.

Absolutely lethal in her leggings and purple sweater.

Weeks of avoiding her—not to mention *years* of rushing home to take care of Jesse and stuffing all the cash I'd earned into a hollowed-out book in my bookcase—and all it took to test my resolve to avoid temptation and keep moving forward was five minutes in the same room as Greer-fucking-Richmond.

If I wanted to stay on at Richmond House, I was going to have to drive her around—it'd been clear from the start of our little business meeting that Sterling wasn't giving me a choice in the matter. I didn't like how he thought he could control me just because he paid well, that he could say "jump" and I'd ask, "how high?" I wasn't a dog. For that reason alone, I'd thought about quitting as soon as he'd started in on the "expansion" of my "scope of duties." Because of Jesse, I was usually only able to work part-time —weekday mornings—but I could probably find another gig to see me through the next few months. Too bad I didn't want to.

"Please, Jace. Mr. Blackwell, I mean."

Jesus Christ. When she'd looked at me and mouthed those words with her bare, pink lips...it was an invitation. A seduction even, though she probably hadn't intended it that way. Either way, I knew I was already fucked. She was only just out of my sight, and I wanted to see her again. I wanted to do a lot more than see her.

If I wasn't trash, if this were my house and if Greer were my girl, I'd have lifted her up and laid her down on the first horizontal surface I could find. Sterling's desk, probably. I'd give her my tongue as I pushed that sweater up and off her body and used it to twist her arms together above her head. Then I'd run my hands up the planes of her smooth stomach and over the full breasts encased in her bra. I'd hook the edges of those lacy cups with my fingers and pull them down—

"Jace!" Eugenia called out. "Hello there, Jace!"

Goddamn it.

I'd been walking toward the tool shed built strategically inside the tree line, hidden from view of the house. Lost in my fantasy, I hadn't noticed Eugenia—wearing the same kind of ridiculous clear poncho I'd seen pictures of tourists wearing at Niagara Falls and carrying a matching umbrella —angling toward me from across the lawn. Now I had to talk to Sterling's...whatever she was to him...with a hard-on.

Great.

"Eugenia," I said cautiously, folding my arms, trying to distract her from what was going on in my jeans.

"I'm glad I caught up to you." She placed her hand on her chest and used the other to fan her face. It was a bit dramatic, considering it was cold out and she'd only walked a few hundred yards downhill. I could see she'd managed to avoid the worst of the mud. "I've wanted to speak with you for some time."

This was new. I'd talked to Eugenia occasionally over the roughly two years I'd worked for Sterling, but she'd never sought me out before. I hoped there wasn't a problem with my work.

"About what?" I asked, sounding harsher than I intended.

"About our darling Greer, of course."

Dangerous AND destined to be a pain in the ass.

"What about her?"

"Sterling and I...we're growing increasingly concerned." Eugenia smoothed down the apron underneath the poncho that covered her dark blue dress.

"I don't understand. Concerned about what, exactly? And why is it my problem?"

She smiled her big, creepy smile. I expected her to call me out for my rudeness, but she didn't.

"Well, it's not my place to judge, but Sterling said she spends most of her time in her bedroom alone. It's not surprising that she doesn't have any friends here yet—she hasn't left the house since she arrived, nor shown any interest in her coursework. I can't imagine you'd be privy to the circumstances surrounding her mother's death, but you should know that Greer is refusing any help in the form of therapy..."

Eugenia trailed off as if wanting me to confirm what I did and didn't know about Greer, but I wasn't going to take the bait. When she'd told me her mother had died, I'd figured it was cancer or something. Had there been an accident? Had she been murdered? Why would Greer need therapy?

"Yeah, sorry, Eugenia, but I'm still wondering what Greer's private life has to do with me."

"I guess we're all just so worried that our darling girl is depressed. But I couldn't help but notice that she perks up whenever she sees you, so I just thought that maybe you two had...formed a connection."

Too bad the only "connection" we had was how badly I wanted her. "Look, I've only talked to her once when she first got here. Well, twice if you count just now."

"Just now?"

"I came from Sterling's office. I'm going to be her ride until she learns how to drive herself around."

Eugenia's smile rarely slipped, but it tightened now, the faint crow's feet around her eyes becoming more pronounced as she fought to maintain a pleasant facial expression. I could see a bit of her bright fuchsia lipstick on one of her front teeth, like she'd rushed to reapply it when she'd seen me coming across the yard. Maybe she was so used to being the puppet master, the first to know everything, that being the last to know didn't compute.

"I see. I'd spoken to Sterling at length about allowing you to become a part of Greer's life. He was very much against it at first, very much against the two of you spending time together in any capacity, but when I explained how it could be beneficial to us...I just didn't realize he'd gone over my head to execute our plan."

"Wait—become a part of her life? What is that supposed to mean? Sterling just asked me to make myself available to drive her when she needed me."

"That, and we're encouraging you to become her friend. Her confidant."

"Sterling didn't say anything about becoming her friend. In fact, I think he'd prefer me not to speak to her at all. Just get her where she needs to go and back safely."

"You let me worry about Sterling," Eugenia snapped. "I'm just saying, when you're driving her around, don't be afraid to show her around town a bit. Engage with her. Listen to what she has to say. And then, we'd like to hear back from you. Just so we know what her plans are. For the future, I mean. And anything she's...discovered...while she's here. We're willing to pay you, of course. We'll pay double for the hours you spend with Greer."

"Let me get this straight. You want to pay me double to spend time with Greer and then tell you what we talked about?"

"You don't have to be so crass. But yes. And if you accept, we'd expect you not to mention our arrangement to her. Sterling and I just want to make sure she's moving on from her childhood traumas in the healthiest ways possible."

I'm sure.

I thought about it. Jesse's drinking had once again landed him in the hospital for the foreseeable future, at least a few weeks, so I'd been able to work full days at Richmond House. In addition to the boats, Sterling had started adding some handyman work, and my money wad was growing fast. Another few thousand bucks, and I'd be set up for my new life. I'd be able to get a nice, new, clean place I could be proud of and hire someone to take care of the old man. I could use my GI Bill for tuition at the local college as well.

"Okay," I said to Eugenia. "But like you said, I don't want Greer ever knowing about this. Ever. She won't hear about it from me, but I don't want you or Sterling running your mouths either."

Eugenia nodded. "I have a few stipulations of my own. First—most importantly—this arrangement is about being a friend to Greer. Not a boyfriend."

I smiled and held up my fingers in a Boy Scout salute.

"Scout's honor," I lied. "Luckily, I'm not exactly boyfriend material."

"I don't recall you ever attending Scouts, Jace Blackwell, but I'll hold you to it. The second condition is that you'll need to be the one to teach Greer how to drive."

My smile faded fast.

8
GREER

The hour passed slowly, the continued heavy rain almost making me wish I hadn't chosen today of all days to venture out of the house. I could be in my bed with the covers pulled over my head—my preferred sleeping position—instead of changing into and back out of at least a dozen outfits, trying to look good for the man Sterling paid to drive me into town.

You're so ridiculous, G. Jace wouldn't acknowledge you, so you asked your grandfather to make him your driver? Pathetic.

I quickly plaited my hair into twin braids and changed back into the high-waisted leggings and purple sweater I'd been wearing to begin with—leggings and a sweater, my Astoria uniform. I topped it with a white rubber raincoat, traded my sneakers for a pair of knee-high, bright-red Hunter wellies, and slung the waterproof backpack I'd asked Eugenia to pick up for me over my shoulder, my laptop safely ensconced inside. The leather backpack I used for school in Seattle was no match for this kind of rain.

I walked around the side of the house from the back door. I hadn't seen Garbage the Goose since his unprovoked attack on the evening I'd arrived, but I was always on high alert. I wasn't sure where to meet Jace, but I figured he'd find me easiest on the front porch. I'd been waiting for ten minutes, well past the hour mark since the tense meeting in Sterling's office, *tap, tap, tapping* away to my heart's content —just this once—when he came around the side of the house and saw me.

"You ready?" he asked. He'd traded in his wool peacoat for a yellow rain slicker he must have found in the shed he mentioned, but I could see the rain had already soaked the hair he hadn't quite managed to cover with his hood.

"Yes!" I called over the porch railing before walking down the wooden steps, careful not to slip and fall into the mud as I made my way over to him.

I couldn't understand what I'd done to make him avoid me. I mean, besides tripping him and messing up his painting project. He probably thought I was some sad orphan who wanted approval from a grandfather who'd lost interest immediately and was now indifferent to her presence. I admit that when I first came to stay, I had a fantasy that my grandfather would be like the businessman in Annie—immediately drawn to my precociousness, taking me with him everywhere he went, and tap dancing through the house with me when we were at home together.

In truth, Sterling was nothing to me but an extremely considerate roommate—so much so that sometimes I forgot we shared a bathroom. Everything was always spotless. I never bothered him, and he never bothered me. He read his newspapers every morning over breakfast, spent most of his time locked in his office, and occasionally went out to meetings. I even saw Oren and Eugenia around the house sometimes, but never for dinner like I had that first night. I ate my dinners alone, usually in my room because Sterling was still working. Everything was always in passing. Everyone just passed me by, and I was as lonely here as I'd been back at home with my mother. Lonelier because she wasn't here to distract me.

Jace's impatient shuffling brought me back to the present moment.

"I meant what I said before. In the office. About you not having to drive your own car."

I offered him the key Oren had given me to the car he'd brought over for me to drive, a 1980s MG, stretching out my cupped hands like I was about to receive a Communion wafer.

"What's that?" he yelled over the sound of the downpour, looking down at the key in my outstretched palms.

"The keys to the car Oren lent me. It's in the garage."

"Why would Oren lend you a car?"

"I don't know. To be nice?"

Jace shook his head and brought his hand up to shield his eyes, peering across the front of the house to the open bay of the detached garage Sterling used to house his cars.

"That an MG?"

"Yes. But don't ask me any other questions about it. I don't know anything about cars."

His mouth stretched into a genuine smile.

"Have you ridden in it yet?"

"No."

"Then I forgive you for not knowing that a man my size would never be comfortable riding in that car. I wouldn't even fit into it, sweetheart."

The time before when he called me "sweetheart," he'd been angry. This time, the word held no bite.

"That's not the car for you, anyway," he went on. "It's

pretty, but it's not the type of vehicle you want to be driving in this weather. And it's a stick..." He rolled his eyes.

I'd honestly never considered Jace's size when I offered him the MG, but I trusted him when he said there was no way he'd be able to sit comfortably inside. As far as his other gripes, beggars couldn't be choosers. "Okay. Well, I could ask Sterling to trade cars for the day, and we can take—"

"Don't bother. We're taking the Bronco." He turned and started across the field toward his ride.

"Oh, *are* we?" I retorted, annoyed at his abrupt bossiness. "Well, okay then. Glad that's been decided." I followed behind him, trying to walk in the path he cut with his large body rather than forge my own through the tall, wet grass.

He opened the heavy passenger door first, gesturing for me to get in before walking around to the other side of the truck. I climbed in and inhaled the concentrated aroma of campfires and clove cigarettes laced with a hint of diesel. Jace's scent.

Like Jimmy Ducky, Jace was all business on the ride to town. I looked out the window and marveled at the towering evergreen forests we passed along the way. The last time I was on this road, I was so nervous I couldn't keep my body from shaking. Now, I felt like I was seeing everything for the first time. The mighty Columbia River was a sea of whitecaps and rolling fog banks as we neared the center of town. I watched a group of seagulls squabbling midflight. Laughing, I looked to Jace, only to find him already watching me, black eyes blazing with intensity. He quickly looked back to the road.

Jace maneuvered the Bronco through the streets of downtown Astoria, pulling smoothly into a space in the library's busy parking lot and shifting up into park.

"How long do you think this will take? I have a lot of shit to do today back at the house."

I frowned. Was he going to be like this every time he drove me anywhere? I know I trapped him into this job, but, for me at least, the trip from Richmond House had been exhilarating. Freeing. Why did he have to be such an asshole?

"It'll take as long as it takes," I replied tartly. He released a heavy sigh. "You don't have to stay here and wait for me in the parking lot. Feel free to run errands or...whatever else you might want to do to pass the time."

Looking me over before lowering his seat, he stretched his large frame out and threw an arm over his eyes. "Or maybe I'll just take a nap. Yeah, I like the idea of getting paid to take a nap."

"Go ahead, then. Makes no difference to me."

I jerked my door open and slid out, spitefully slamming it behind me before making a run for it through the rain to the doors of Astoria's downtown library branch.

Housed in a historic Art Deco building just off Commercial Street, the library's interior sprawled backward almost an entire city block from its entryway. Its soaring ceiling created a cavernous effect. The fiction and nonfiction sections ran along opposite walls, while an adorable children's area in the center of the space featured a dozen or more miniature chairs in bright, rainbow colors. Around the perimeter of the great room were alcoves stuffed with mismatched furniture—tables for researching, comfortable chairs, even the occasional beanbag. The space was both eclectic and charming.

I settled into a damask armchair with a footrest someone had placed at the end of a long stack of titles in the fiction section, partially hidden from view. Before I fired up my computer, I fished my phone out of my backpack—

dead. I hadn't bothered to charge it, and now I couldn't check my texts. But I probably didn't have any. I didn't have any friends, and Sterling was my only family, so who would be texting me? I threw the phone back into the mix at the bottom of the bag before opening my laptop and navigating to the only tab bookmarked in my browser—*University of Washington Spring Quarter 2014 Historical Research Project Requirements (Remote)*.

I'd registered for my spring-quarter classes before my mother had died, well before I'd received Sterling's slightly coerced invitation to visit him, but I'd been able to work with the Office of Registration to drop those classes and pick up a remote research course for credit. My schedule come fall might be a bit on the heavy side, but I was still on track for graduation.

After reading through the requirements several times— weekly assignments designed to teach different modern-day researching techniques, and a thesis paper and recorded presentation due no later than June 14 on a lesser-known historical event that had impacted a local region in ways good or bad—I was sure the wreck of the *Jonathan Richmond* was a good match. I'd never seen it in person, but I knew the wreck was still visible during the summer months out on the beach. If nothing else, it had brought tourists to the area for the past hundred fifty years or so.

I clicked on the Week One assignment link.

Welcome to the University of Washington's Spring Quarter 2014 Historical Research Project! Your first assignment is to create an account on Ancestry.com and begin an online family tree.

Thanks to Eugenia, I knew the Richmonds came from England not long before Richmond House was built. At least I had *some* information to go off. The better part of two hours flew past while I created my Ancestry.com account as instructed and filled in what meager details I knew about my mother and Sterling. I looked at the blank spaces that made up my father's side of the tree for a long time before I closed my laptop.

Reluctant to return to the Bronco and subject myself to Jace's sour mood—no matter how justified—I wandered over to the nonfiction side of the library. I'd spent a lot of time in libraries as a girl, trying to understand my mother's illness, and I quickly found the section housing the Dewey decimal number I knew by heart. *616.8526. Eating Disorders.*

Recognizing several titles I'd read before, I touched their spines reverently and pulled one off the shelf, allowing myself to think about my mother for the first time since the night she'd gone to sleep and hadn't woken up. I thought again of her death mask in the bedroom mirror, how quickly I'd pushed the memory away, and I suddenly felt cold.

"Ready to go?"

I yelped in surprise, dropping the book. I watched the corner hit Jace's toe before it bounced to a stop on the carpet. He reached down to pick it up, absorbing the cover with his dark eyes as he straightened.

"*Slow Starve to Victory: A Study of the Anorexic Mind,*" he read aloud. "What is this?"

"It's a book, obviously." I snatched it from his hands and placed it back on the shelf in front of me. It was a bit of an overreaction, but I needed to shut down the inevitable line of questioning. I just didn't want to talk about it right now. "And yes, I'm ready to leave."

"What the fuck, Greer?" he asked, raising his voice slightly above what was acceptable in a public library. "Do you have an eating disorder or something?"

"Lower your voice," I hissed, furious at the escalation when all I wanted was for him to let it go. "That's such a ridiculous conclusion to jump to just because I was holding a book in my hands."

Look at me—do I look like I have an eating disorder?

I turned and booked it toward the double doors at the entrance of the library, so ready to go back to the house and be done with this conversation. But it was too late. My mind flooded with dozens of other phrases I'd heard my mother say in the years before she died.

"Greasy fries or skinny thighs, Greer?"

"Bigger snacks mean bigger slacks, Greer."

"Nobody said it was easy, Greer."

My eyes welled with unshed tears as I sunk into a river of old conversations I'd rather not remember. I barely made it past the doors before the tears I'd been holding back dripped down my cheeks, and a series of racking sobs escaped my tight chest. I wrapped my arms around myself and felt Jace come up behind me.

"Greer, if you're sick, you should tell me. I want to help you."

I sniffed and let out a cynical laugh. "Oh, yeah? You want to help me? Since when?"

"Since now."

"Then how about you help me by driving me back. You don't know anything about anything, and I'm too tired to get into it right now."

"You don't have to explain anything. Why would you just happen to be in the eating disorder section of the library looking at a book about anorexia?"

"You seriously think I have anorexia?" I challenged him. "I don't."

"Then why were you looking at that book?"

"None of your damn business!"

The rain had slowed during the hours I'd been inside, and I just wanted to get back to the comfort of my bedroom. That's what I got for lusting after a man who didn't want me. Thankfully, I considered myself cured. I took off through the heavy mist toward the Bronco.

9
JACE

I followed her to the rig, easily outpacing her to the passenger door and opening it. The rain wasn't coming down as heavily anymore, but it was still cold, damp, and the parking lot pavement was slick with puddles.

"Do you seriously not bother to lock your car doors here?" she asked. "How stupid."

You have no idea how stupid I can be.

I was starting to pick up on the fact that when Greer was angry, she went on the offensive. I didn't respond. I shut her in, then took my time walking around to my door. I'd spent the first hour she was gone napping in the truck and the rest of the time popping into a few of the seedier bars nearby. I was looking for my mother. Sometimes I'd run into her at a bar, and she'd give me a sloppy hug and shed a few tears while she told me how handsome I was. It wasn't much in the way of motherly love, but I was in the mood to see her. Let her hug me. Tell her about my job and maybe about Greer—not that there was anything to tell. But I couldn't find her today.

I looked at Greer through the front windshield. She was

staring out the side window, arms wrapped around her body. I didn't know what to think. On one hand, she was right. It was none of my business. Up until a few hours ago, I'd been trying my best not to get involved with her or anyone else. I didn't know her, had never seen her eat or not eat. She was slender, but it seemed to fit her frame. She didn't look sick. So, what was it to me?

On the other hand, I'd be lying if I said I couldn't see how lonely she was. I was in the room when Sterling—a man who was supposed to care about her—had delivered that scathing put-down earlier. Where was her father? Where was her support system? Was Sterling really the only family she had?

I got into the Bronco just in time—the spatter of rain picked up again, and we sat in silence, listening to the drops on the windshield. Maybe I should start over, try again to talk to her.

"I know we don't really know each other," I said. "But you can talk to me if you want."

"I tried being nice to you, and you made it a point to never even look in my direction. Why the hell would I talk to you now?"

I clenched my fists in frustration before turning my head to look her square in the eyes.

"I know. I'm sorry. I just didn't want to get involved in anything, especially with you."

"First of all, who was asking you to? Second of all, 'especially with me'? What's that supposed to mean?"

"It's supposed to mean...I don't know. It doesn't matter."

"It matters to me!" She was practically shrieking now, her carefully controlled emotions in ruins after I'd callously ripped open her wounds without even realizing it. "When I told you before about my mother, you couldn't have cared less. What if your mother had died? Huh? What if your mother was ugly and damaged, but you still loved her because she was your mother, but then even she abandoned you? Would you care then?"

My hands shook as I started the car. I wanted to peel out of the parking lot at top speed and fly through town, but it was dangerous in the wet weather. I had Greer in the car, and I needed to keep her safe, even though she'd just crossed the line and said some stupid shit that made me mad as hell.

She didn't mean it like that. It's your own fault she doesn't know anything about you.

We bumped along in silence across town to the peninsula where Richmond House loomed large at the peak. I pulled up to the field just before dark, barely turning off the car and putting it in park before I was out the door and across the field to the porch and sat down on the steps. I had a few more things to do before I called it a day, but I wasn't sure our conversation was over.

She followed me, sitting down beside me as gracefully as she could in her squeaky boots and heavy jacket.

"Look, I'm sorry I lost my temper, okay?" she said after a few beats. "I didn't mean to yell at you. Since I got here, all I've wanted was to be more than strangers. We got off to a bad start, but I'm willing to set everything aside and be friends. I'd like it if we were."

I turned my head to look at her, and she graced me with a dazzling smile. Even though her eyes were red and puffy from crying, her features were stunning. Vulnerable. How easy it would be for me to open my arms. To be a shoulder for her to cry on, and when she was done crying, to touch my lips gently to her full, pink mouth. How easily could her sweetness soothe my anger, smooth off the rough edges of my soul? Too bad I was never going to find out. Just like in

Sterling's office this morning, I knew what I needed to do. My damp hair clung to the back of my neck as I turned my mouth up into the slightly cruel, slightly sardonic smile many a woman knew so well. I spoke softly.

"I'd bet anything you get a lot of compliments, Greer Richmond. I'd bet everyone just lines up to tell you how mature you are. How generous. How beautiful."

Daring her to look away, I moved my face closer and closer like I was going to kiss her. I could almost hear her heart pounding in her frozen body before it flashed splotchy heat throughout her chest and neck. When my face was close enough that I could inhale her breath, I stopped. My hand reached down and found the end of a long braid. I tugged on it gently, tipping her head to the side, before playfully kissing the tip of her nose.

"The problem is, I'm not nearly as mature as you. Not generous at all. Definitely not as beautiful. If I were you, I'd keep my distance. I wouldn't want you to get hurt playing a game you're not any good at."

I pushed myself up off the steps and walked around the side of the house without a backward glance.

I headed for the tool shed, prepared to make up for the way I'd tossed things around while I was in a hurry to meet Greer earlier.

You couldn't fucking wait to be alone with her.

Yeah, but now that I'd effectively killed whatever might have been, I wasn't worried about that anymore. Turning the corner, I stopped in my tracks at the sight of Sterling sitting calmly in a ritzy lawn chair he'd pulled out for the occasion. Legs crossed, wool coat buttoned, holding an umbrella perfectly straight above his head despite being under the eaves of the shed, it struck me how different it looked when Jesse sat relaxing on the lawn.

"Mr. Blackwell," he greeted me as I approached.

"Mr. Richmond. What are you doing out here? I mean, it's your house, you can sit wherever you want, but..."

"I saw your car and realized I needed to speak with you before you left. Despite the fact that you seemed quite... comfortable...inside," an obvious reference to my lack of footwear at our meeting earlier today—I tried not to roll my eyes—"I would rather Greer not be privy to our conversation."

"If this is about Greer, I drove her to the library and then straight home," I said, suddenly paranoid that Sterling had been watching us on the porch, even though there's no way he could have been in two places at once.

"I'm not inquiring as to her whereabouts. I merely wanted to check in and see if she'd mentioned anything unusual during your alone time together today."

"Unusual?"

"Anything...private. Anything that might destroy the reputation the family has worked for hundreds of years to cultivate."

Woah. What the fuck? I thought he just wanted to make sure she was happy.

"I..."

"Let me remind you that your paycheck for this afternoon's excursion depends on the sharing of information."

"Okay. Just let me think. I went in to get her in the library, and she was reading a book on...eating disorders."

Tattling on Greer felt shitty, but it's not like she'd opened up to me and told me any of her secrets. I was just reporting what I saw. Sterling's face remained expressionless. I plowed on. "So maybe you guys should think about getting her some help?"

"Greer doesn't have an eating disorder. Clearly."

The fuck does that mean?

"That was her mother," he went on, showing a

complete lack of emotion at his own daughter's struggles. "Her sickness eventually took her life, and that's likely why Greer was researching. I haven't known the girl for long, but she has a penchant for knowledge. She seeks it out."

Her mother. Now I felt even worse. I shouldn't have accused her.

"Anything else?" Sterling asked.

"No, sir. I confronted her...about the book...and now she's angry with me." At least I assumed she was. I hadn't stuck around to assess the damage I'd inflicted with my rejection.

"Well, I expect you to turn that around as soon as possible. It's imperative that we encourage Greer to find her way into the next chapter in her life without inflicting any damage on what we've worked so hard to shore up here."

It felt like he was talking in riddles. Sterling wanted Greer gone, that much was obvious. Traumas ran like blood-red ribbons through many of the families that called this remote, rocky coastline home—I knew that better than anyone. The question was whether Sterling wanted to protect Greer, or whether he saw her as a threat.

I just nodded my head in response.

10
GREER

Not any good at? Not any good at?
Jace's words continued to knock around in my mind, fueling my anger and embarrassment.

"A game you're not any good at?" How the hell would he know what I was good at? I'm great at games. The best.

And Jace Blackwell was about to find out. After our bizarre exchange on the porch yesterday, I expected him to go back to avoiding me. When he couldn't—when he had to take me back to the library, for example—I assumed he'd revert to one of his emotional default settings of brooding anger or smirking condescension. But I didn't care. Not anymore. How dare he yell at me about a book I was holding inside a public library. How dare he start asking me a million personal questions when he wasn't willing to answer any pertaining to himself. How dare he trigger that landslide of memories that led me to say things I regretted. Still, after all that, I'd decided to be the bigger person. I'd offered an olive branch. He'd rejected it. Fine. "Over it" didn't even begin to describe how I felt about Jace Blackwell at the moment.

So, I was surprised when he approached me this morning as I came out of the garage where I'd been admiring the MG Oren kept insisting was mine. The rain had stopped sometime during the night, replaced by a stiff breeze that rocked the trees surrounding the house back and forth.

"Hey," he said, walking toward me, boots crunching through the crushed oyster shells someone—presumably him—had begun shoveling around the property and down the tracks to help solidify all the mud.

"Oh, hey," I returned coldly.

Yesterday, I'd been too cold, too wet, too shaken to wonder where he'd gone or even watch him go. As soon as he'd turned his back on me, I'd walked swiftly in the opposite direction toward the back door, wanting to escape to my room where I could lock the door, change into dry clothes, and be alone with my thoughts.

Your obsessive thoughts.

I realized now that I hadn't taken the time to process my mother's death. What happened with Jace showed how defensive I was. I hadn't been in the right headspace to tell him about my mother even if I eventually wanted to—and I wasn't sure I did. It didn't matter anymore. His opinion of me didn't matter. I was here to find out who my father was and why my mother hated my grandfather so much. So far, I didn't have a clue, so I resolved to concentrate on my research project and at the very least receive the credits I needed to close out the year.

"I just wanted to say first off that I should've accepted your apology last night and your offer to be friends, instead of being a smart-ass," he said.

"Well, unfortunately for you, that was a one-time offer."

"Figured." He smiled at my sassiness. "Since it's too late for that, would you be willing to hear an apology from me?"

No. But I nodded. The sooner he said his piece, the sooner he'd be gone.

"I'm sorry about the way I reacted in the library yesterday. Even if I thought...I just shouldn't have handled things the way I did."

"And what about all that stuff you said on the porch?"

"Sorry, sweetheart. Meant every word of that. You should stay away from me if you know what's good for you."

Cue eyeroll.

"I can't. You're my driver, remember?"

"Speaking of, you planning to go back to the library this week?" he asked.

"I was hoping to go tomorrow."

"I'll be here working. You can just come find me, or... how about on the days you need a ride, you put something in your window? Like something bright that I can see from the field. Then I'll know I need to quit early. Maybe we could meet on the porch at, like, two o'clock on those days?"

"Sounds like a plan," I said, looking past him to the forest beyond.

What was *that?*

"What are you looking at?" He turned around and scanned the woods behind him.

"Nothing. I just thought I saw a flash of...something. A streak of white and a girl or a woman or something. Or a small man."

"No small men up here," he said matter-of-factly. "The only women on the peninsula are you and Eugenia. And Anna, forgot about her."

"Anna?" I'd thrown a trench coat on over my sweater before I'd headed to the garage this morning. It came almost to my knees, but it wasn't nearly warm enough to block the wind whipping my hair around. I absently played with the sash, tying a triple knot before I forced my hands to be still.

"Eugenia's daughter. She's a year younger than I am. I remember her from school."

"Oh, I think my grandfather mentioned her once. I didn't know Eugenia was married."

Jace cocked his head to the side and scratched his scalp underneath his thick hair.

"Yeah, she's not, but I don't think I should say any more about it than that."

"Umm...okay. Why?"

"Because I'm not going to get even more involved in your family's drama than I already am. Ask Sterling if you're so curious."

"Ask him about what?"

Jace sighed. "My dad said something when I was younger about some rumors about who Anna's father was. Okay? That's all I know."

"Do your parents live in Astoria?" I asked, glomming onto the mention of his father.

He scrubbed his hands down his face in frustration the same way he did the first time we met when I went to sit down next to him on the boat. The wind picked up again; the sound of tree limbs snapping made it hard for me to hear him.

"Yeah, they're both around. You're pretty nosy, you know that?"

"I could say the same thing about you. You sure didn't have a problem asking me a bunch of super-personal questions yesterday. And by asking, I mean 'demanding to know in the loudest voice possible.'"

"I said I was sor—"

"You know what, it's fine." I crossed my arms over my chest in a hug. "I'm over it. I just thought we were having a decent conversation for once, so I thought I'd take the opportunity to learn a bit more about you. You don't have to talk about your family if you don't want to."

His black eyes searched mine, and for once, he was the one to look away first. He kept his eyes on his boots.

"I've got nothing to hide. I'm not ashamed of where I started, but just know you might not like what you hear about me."

It wasn't the response I expected.

"I don't have anything to hide either," I echoed. "I just..." Once again, my eyes filled with tears, and I forced the last few words out on a tide of emotion. He stood there awkwardly and shoved his hands into the back pockets of his jeans. For the first time since I met him, he wasn't pushing me away. He wasn't angry. We were finally connecting, though I didn't understand over what. Not yet. "It's just hard," I continued, "to talk about."

"I know."

Then he turned and walked away. I'd set out wanting to crack Jace Blackwell's armor, but I was the one who felt exposed in the end. I stood for a moment and thought about what he'd said about the rumors surrounding Anna's parentage. I'd finally stumbled across the kind of family gossip that could bring me closer to discovering the secrets my mother had kept from me. I decided to go straight to Sterling before I lost my nerve.

After discarding my mud-caked boots and trench coat in the back-door pantry, I slipped my shoes back on and walked along the wide rug from the back of the house to the front and knocked on the door to his office.

"Enter."

I stepped inside, balancing on my toes so my heels wouldn't sink into the soft, aged hardwood and leave marks.

"Good morning, Sterling."

"Greer. Is everything all right?"

"Everything is fine. I just wanted to ask you sort of an...odd question."

He waited for me to go on.

"I was talking to...some people I met in town...and someone told me that Eugenia had a daughter but that she's never been married."

"Who in town was talking about that?"

"I don't know. I didn't catch their names," I lied. "But they knew who I was, and they told me about Eugenia's daughter."

"*I* told you when you first arrived that Eugenia had a daughter. Her name is Anna."

"Yes, I remember that now. Do you...know her?"

"Of course I do. She lived here—for a time. She was just...exceptional. She was an exquisitely beautiful little girl. So delicate. Like your mother." He cleared his throat. "But then she grew up. She still lives on the peninsula. She works in a bookstore downtown."

"It sounds like you two were close. When she was little, I mean. When she lived here."

"I find the innocence of youth to be the most sacred thing in the world," he said, shifting in his seat, his eyes bright. "'Children are the hands by which we take hold of heaven.' Do you know who wrote that, Greer?"

"Um...no."

"It was Henry Ward Beecher. He was a minister. You'd do well to study his works."

Okay...

"But Eugenia was never married?" I asked. "The people I spoke with told me there was some sort of controversy."

"Greer, please. I don't see that Eugenia having a baby out of wedlock twenty-five years ago has anything to do with you. You're welcome to ask her about it yourself, though I wouldn't recommend it. Eugenia is very particular about the subjects she deems appropriate for conversation between acquaintances."

He gestured toward the door, indicating that he was through answering my questions. But I was on to something. Like the mist coming off the river, I could feel it in my bones.

∾

STERLING WAS HIS USUAL SELF THE FOLLOWING MORNING AT breakfast, sipping his coffee and reading his newspapers. As always, I smiled politely, ate very little, and excused myself at the first opportunity, nicking a roll of Scotch tape from Eugenia's household supply cupboard before heading back up the stairs. Jace wanted a sign? It just so happened I was prepared to deliver.

Back in my room, I searched my underwear drawer for my most scandalous pair, the pair all women pick up at one time or another but rarely wear. Neon yellow and impossibly tiny, a set of triple straps on both sides of the thong connected the front to the back.

Are you sure you want to do this, G? What if he takes it the wrong way?

He wouldn't, I decided, tearing off two long strips of the Scotch tape. It was just a funny prank. I taped the panties to the window using a giant "x."

How's that for 'something in your window,' Jace Blackwell?

Between the uneasy truce I'd formed with Jace, Sterling's rose-colored memories of Anna as a girl setting off alarm bells on the family-secrets front, and the research due for my research project, I felt heavy. I needed some comic relief.

I stood well back from the windows as Jace pulled up in the Bronco. Eight in the morning like clockwork. He swung out of the cab and walked toward the field, glancing up at the house. And froze. I couldn't see his face clearly from that distance, but as he began walking toward the house, it was clear he was torn between laughter and disbelief. After a few minutes spent trudging through the field, he was directly under my window, looking up. He scrubbed his hand over his face and shook his head back and forth before heading toward the tool shed. He shot a peace sign over his shoulder—or maybe he wanted to remind me that we were meeting at two.

I untaped my panties from the window before Eugenia —or worse, Sterling—saw them, throwing them back into the drawer and putting on my raincoat before locking my bedroom door behind me and pocketing the key. On my way down the stairs, I spotted Oren exiting Sterling's office.

"Oren!"

He gave me a warm smile. "Hello, Greer. How's the MG?"

"It's great, but I still haven't gotten the chance to drive it. Thank you so much for loaning it to me. That was so kind."

"It's my pleasure. The car is yours if you want it. It's just taking up space in my garage."

"I'll...think about it."

"Fair enough. And how are you settling in?"

"It's been...okay. It's only been a few weeks, but I've enjoyed getting to know my grandfather." I gave a diplomatic answer.

"I'm so glad to hear that. When Sterling first mentioned you were coming, I was worried that you'd be bored here or...unhappy somehow. Many of the young women who've lived here since I've been around mentioned at one time or another that life here can be quite...isolating."

"Yes, but it's also cozy. It's a break from the chaos of the outside world, that's for sure. Listen," I said, lowering my voice, "I'm glad I ran into you. I was wondering if I could ask you some questions about something Sterling doesn't seem to know much about."

"But of course. Shall we retire to the parlor?"

"I thought you'd never ask." I smiled, playing along with his formality.

We sat down on the two identical velvet chaise lounges facing each other in the middle of the large double room. Many parts of the house were worn and dusty from disuse, but the parlor had been meticulously cleaned. I knew I should offer Oren coffee, or tea, or refreshments of some kind, but I didn't want to go scrounging in Eugenia's kitchen. If she was here, I didn't want her coming in to serve us.

"So..." I began.

"So. What did you want to ask me about?"

"It's...sort of awkward. I told Sterling that there were people at the library who told me what I'm about to tell you, but really, it was Jace."

"Blackwell? Well, if it's town gossip, he's as good a source as any. He's lived here all his life."

"He has?"

"Yes, born and raised. I remember seeing him around town as a child on his bike. His skin was dark enough that I wondered whether he wouldn't be more comfortable on a reservation, but come to find out, there is no reservation near Astoria. Can you believe that? Anyway, not a lot of parental supervision, I'm afraid, in that household. Seems to be a decent sort now, though. Sterling's very happy with his work."

My mind was spinning. Jace was Native American? I guess it made sense, considering how gorgeous and angular his features were paired with his copper skin and ink-black hair and eyes. I had more questions about Jace, but they would have to wait.

"Yeah, so anyway, Jace told me that Eugenia has a daughter named Anna, who's around his age."

"That's right," he said with a smile, but his voice suddenly sounded a bit hollow.

"He said Eugenia has never been married, and something about how his father told him there was some drama surrounding it having to do with my family?"

Oren sat still on the chaise, hands folded on his knee. The number of seconds ticking down made it evident that he knew what I was talking about but didn't want to discuss it.

"What exactly did Sterling tell you?" he finally asked.

"That it was none of my business. And it isn't, only I'm trying to figure out what it was like in the house when my mother was growing up. I need to know why she was so quick to run away. How she got so sick."

"My dear, knowing that won't bring her back."

"I know. But I still need to know."

He leaned forward, looking into my eyes, his blue irises so unlike the warm brown of Sterling's and my mother's. And mine.

"Okay," he said on a loud exhale. "I guess you'd find out eventually in any case. I can tell you that the rumors surrounding Anna's birth have to do with Eugenia's living here at the time, along with your grandmother and your mother. Blair was, I think, thirteen when Anna was born."

"So, for her, it was like having a baby sister?"

"Yes and no. This is all secondhand, of course. Sterling and I didn't form our business alliance until your mother was years older. But I understand that, growing up, Sterling doted on Blair from the moment she was born. Sterling and your grandmother occupied the adjoining master suites upstairs, and Blair's crib was in Sterling's bedroom, not hers. By the time she was a toddler, Sterling had created a small office desk for her and set it up in the corner of his office. He took her everywhere with him—meetings, weekend trips. They spent so much time together that it raised more than a few eyebrows. Folks thought the way he...interacted...with her was...inappropriate—especially out in public—but it tapered off enough once she reached adolescence that nothing came of the gossip. Blair was the apple of Sterling's eye. That is, until Anna was born."

A sick feeling of dread snaked its way through my stomach. I'd never met her, but suddenly, I hated Anna. I hated the woman who'd stolen my grandfather's affection from my mother, especially when I knew what Anna didn't—that it had cost her everything. That it had cost her life.

"Eugenia was living on the third floor at the time, and no one knew she was even pregnant. Suddenly, there was an infant in the house, and I guess Sterling took to her the same way he'd taken to Blair thirteen years before."

"And he just cast my mom to the side."

"When I met your mother, she was clearly struggling. She and Sterling barely spoke, and when they did, it was clear that Sterling was indifferent. Blair, bless her heart, she just kept trying to please him. But no matter what she did, she couldn't."

"She had an eating disorder. Did you know that?"

"Everyone suspected. But it isn't the sort of thing you can come out and ask someone."

Unless your name is Jace Blackwell, apparently.

"What about Anna's father? What was the controversy?"

Oren lowered his voice. "Now *that* I saw unfold firsthand. It happened years later, just days before your mother left the house for good. Your grandmother, God rest her soul, became suspicious that Sterling and Eugenia had been having an affair and that Anna, who was five years old at the time, was Sterling's biological child."

I inhaled slowly, digesting the shocking story, anxiety writhing in my belly. Oren, who'd been leaning closer and closer to me as the story unfolded suddenly straightened.

"Is she?" I asked.

"I don't know. I don't know if it was ever proven or disproven. All I know is that Eugenia and Anna moved out the following day, at your grandmother's insistence, and then your mother just days later."

Even though I already knew the answer, I made myself ask. "Who told my grandmother about Sterling's alleged affair?"

Oren looked at me with sympathy.

"I'm sorry, but it was your mother. It was Blair."

II
JACE

I watched Greer leave Richmond House from my vantage point crouched beside the 31-foot Chris-Craft Roamer I was working on in the field. She managed to slide one of the massive front wooden doors open just enough to step through sideways before she turned and used her body weight to pull it shut behind her. She was dressed for the weather today in a white coat that looked warmer than the one she'd had on the last time I'd seen her.

It wasn't supposed to rain today, so I was free to work out in the open. When it rained, I had to restrict myself to whatever small project I could take on standing under the blue canopy I'd put up near the house. I'd been working on the Roamer for more than a year, mainly in a slip in the garage since she was the biggest, "nicest" piece-of-shit yacht Sterling had managed to find to date, but I'd pulled her out today. I'd felt a bit confined lately, and I wanted to suck in a few deep lungfuls of cold, salty air while I had the chance before the next spring deluge.

I watched Greer cross the porch, but instead of bouncing away to wherever she was headed, she sat down on the top step and slid her hands under her thighs. She touched her forehead to her knees. The ends of her long hair trailed around in the breeze. She began to rock back and forth, back and forth, back and forth, then stopped. Then, she started again.

What's up with that, sweetheart?

It wasn't the first time I'd noticed her tapping her fingers and toes or moving her body in patterns. It was subtle, but noticeable once you were around her for any length of time.

I looked at my watch. There was no way it was two o'clock already. I could tell something was wrong, but I didn't want to interrupt her private moment when she had no idea I was even out here. It wasn't like that between us.

Instead, I straightened and looked over the Roamer's railing, eyeing the space that would soon house the motor I'd taken apart on the tarp at my feet. I'd taken this boat down to its bare hull until only the bulkheads remained and then built her back up with seven coats of epoxy, primed and painted. I'd replaced every through hull, wire, electrical panel, and all her electronics. Now all that was left was the installation of the Cummins motor. And a good paint job.

I'd learned everything I knew about boats from Jesse—and my stint in the navy, of course. Honestly, I didn't really like working with my hands, building things, but before Greer came to Richmond House, I didn't think much about my work here. I only cared when I was getting paid and how much. But she had me thinking about the future and what I really wanted to do with my life. How I might someday be worthy of someone like her.

I'd dreaded seeing her those first couple of weeks because I knew she wanted my attention, and I couldn't allow myself to reciprocate. That moment on the porch when I'd kissed her nose and tried to scare her away, when

I'd tried to sever whatever bit of connection I'd begun to feel for her when I realized we were both missing the one person in our lives we truly needed—that moment had backfired.

I'd thought about her pretty regularly before, but now all I saw was her face close to mine, how her head had moved when I'd tugged her braid. I'd jumped out of bed, stoked to come to work this morning because I wanted to see her. A relationship was still out of the question—she'd leave me behind in a heartbeat once she got a better offer, and I needed to get my life on track—but I wasn't sure she wanted a casual fling, either. Living in the house alone with Sterling...it didn't take a genius to figure out she was alone and vulnerable. I didn't know what she wanted from me. Or if she even wanted anything.

I was shocked when I pulled up and noticed those panties in the window. It was cute and funny and sexy as hell, and it definitely got my attention. I knew she'd meant it as a joke, but I'd spent the past two hours imagining her wearing those panties and all the ways I could take them off her.

I knelt on the blue tarp, enjoying the familiar crackle beneath me, and spent a few minutes organizing the dismantled engine parts, checking that each was still clean and functional before I started putting them back together. I got so into it I didn't hear Greer approach.

"Hi," she said into my left ear.

I looked up, dropping the fuel injection pump I'd been holding directly onto my kneecap.

"Fuck!"

"Sorry! Are you okay?"

I rubbed my knee hard and kept my mouth shut. It fucking hurt, but I wasn't about to start complaining in front of a gorgeous woman.

"It's fine." I stood up on the tarp and shoved my hands in my back pockets. "Everything okay with you?" I noticed her eyes were puffy and red the way they'd been when I'd driven her home from the library. When they were wet like this, I noticed they turned from honey to dark mahogany, like the wood accents I'd noticed inside Richmond House.

"Not really, but I...can we just not talk about it? It's just family stuff."

I was curious, but I didn't want to spook her. I knew she hadn't found out about my arrangement with Sterling and Eugenia because she hadn't kicked me in the balls yet. The more I thought about what I'd agreed to, the less I wanted to honor the arrangement. Based on our earlier conversation, Sterling couldn't care less about Greer's well-being. It wasn't about that. It was about guarding the Richmond secrets until Greer packed up and left town.

Fuck that.

"It's cool. Look, are you wanting to go to the library early? Because it'll take me an hour or so to get everything back into the garage, but we can go after that."

"No, two is fine. I know you're busy. I just...don't want to be alone right now. I was wondering if I could stay and watch you work?"

Hell yes, sweetheart.

"It's not that exciting. I'm just checking engine parts and putting everything back together."

"Just putting an engine back together, huh? That *does* sound boring," she quipped. "But like I said, I could use the company. Can I stay?"

"Sure. If you want to," I said, smiling at her.

Smiling? Christ.

She seated herself on the corner of the tarp, well away from all the parts, and brought her knees up to her chest. My mind went blank. I picked up the pump but for the life of me couldn't figure out what to do with it. I didn't care. I just wanted to talk to her.

"How long have you been working on Sterling's boats?" she asked, saving me from the awkwardness.

"Few years. My dad had a fishing boat when I was little that was always breaking down. He used to let me help him fix it, hold the flashlight, and whatever. Little things. Until I was big enough to do the repairs on my own."

"Can I ask you something personal?"

"You can *ask*."

"I was talking to Oren just now, and he told me that you're Native American."

"Half. My mother is a member of the Kathlamet Tribe. Chinook Nation."

"That's interesting."

"Not really. We used to do stuff with the Tribe growing up, but since my mom..." I trailed off.

Shut the fuck up, Blackwell.

She'd feel sorry for me, and I didn't want her pity. Didn't need it. Didn't deserve it.

"Well, you sure know a lot about boats," she said awkwardly, sensing that the conversation about my mother was over and wanting to fill the silence.

"Can I ask *you* something personal?"

"Okay," she said uneasily, her face suddenly pale. "What?"

"Why do you call them boats?"

"Wha...what should I be calling them?"

"Ships, sweetheart. Boats are for boys. Ships are for men." I gave her a cocky wink.

"Stop it," she said, laughing, her face relaxing in the wake of my teasing. Obviously, she thought I was going to ask her something she didn't want to answer.

"So, do you want to, like, be a mechanic? Or a painter for a company or something?"

I felt my jaw tighten with irritation. Was that all she thought I could do? Be a laborer my whole life?

Relax. She thinks you enjoy it, and she's just making conversation.

I thought carefully about what I wanted to say. "I do like it, but I've known a lot of men who worked manual labor, and they always end up broken and alone in their forties or fifties. I'm actually saving up for college."

"That's great!" she said, excited. "My classes were such an escape for me when..."

She suddenly looked down and played with the two thin gold rings on her right hand. Her nails were painted a deep navy blue. "What do you want to study?"

I let the obvious change of subject pass. She didn't know I knew about her mom, and I wanted her to tell me herself. We were both playing a game, holding back our truths. But I knew the dam would burst eventually—when she was ready. When I was. "I'm not sure yet. I was thinking law, of becoming a lawyer. If you understand the law well, you can really make an impact on people's everyday lives. If not that, maybe something to do with history."

I liked watching the History Channel at home in the trailer, even though I had to shell out extra money every month for cable. I guess you could say it was my one splurge since I didn't have a cell phone and didn't eat out. I paid for gas, groceries, utilities for the trailer, and the History Channel. And the occasional tattoo. Jesse liked the History Channel too. He and I could sit for hours, side by side, watching shows on everything from World War II to ancient alien civilizations.

"What would you do with a degree in history?"

"Probably become a teacher. I know it's weird considering how I dropped out, but I did like school. I liked some of my teachers there."

"Why did you drop out?"

"What are you studying in school?" This time, I changed the subject.

"Journalism. Why did you drop out?"

I took a deep breath and let it back out. I was enjoying our conversation, enjoying getting to know her better, and she wasn't going to let this go. Journalism. I smiled at her persistent line of questioning. *Of course.*

"I dropped out because my dad's an alcoholic. Like a cirrhosis-of-the-liver alcoholic, and he can't take care of himself on his own. Well, physically, he *could*. But he won't. He'd just drink all day and forget to take his meds."

"Are you still caring for him?"

"Yeah. Only he's in the hospital again, so I have extra time to work for Sterling."

I waited to see the look of pity in her eyes. When it didn't appear, I looked for disgust, but she just fixed her eyes on a spot over my shoulder and didn't say anything.

"Uhhh...Greer?"

"Sorry! I just had an idea."

"What?"

"You know how you're driving me to the library today?"

"Yeah..."

"Do you know what I'm doing there?"

Reading books on eating disorders? "Not exactly. School stuff?"

"I'm working on a research project to earn credits to finish my junior year. It's a historical research project. I had to pick an event from history that's had a significant impact on a local region."

"That's great," I said, genuinely interested. "That's the sort of stuff I hope I'm able to do once I'm back in school."

"I saw this model in the house here. The boat—ship—was named after my family, and since it sank in Astoria, I decided to focus my project on—"

"Are you talking about the *Jonathan Richmond*?"

"Yes! Do you know it?"

Did I know it?

The *Jonathan Richmond* was one of the most famous shallow-water shipwrecks on the West Coast. Local historians still didn't know much about the cargo, about who or what was on board. There weren't any books detailing the events of the wreck—at least not in the local library—but the bones of the actual ship were still visible at low tide out on Clatsop Spit. It was a big tourist attraction in the summer.

"Yeah, I know it. That's going to make for a really cool project."

"I was wondering if…instead of napping in the car…you wanted to work on it with me? There's going to be a lot of research. We could be, like, lab partners. Only at the library."

"Research partners?" I asked, finding her fucking adorable.

"Yes! Research partners. So, you're in?"

Getting closer to Greer while talking about history? It sounded like a dream come true.

"Sure, sweetheart. Why not?"

∽

We rolled into the library parking lot at two thirty, and I snagged us a small table in a front corner next to the "Local

Author" display while Greer used the restroom. The place was pretty packed for a Wednesday afternoon.

She came back and set up her laptop, and together we watched a video made by the professor overseeing the thirty or so students working on their projects remotely this year.

Professor Leipziger stood behind a podium on a lecture stage. A podium.

Pretentious dick.

He talked about the continuation of the class's family tree assignment as if suspended in a perpetual state of keynote address or political rally. Clean-shaven and wearing a purple sweater vest, he was pretty young for a professor. At the end of the video, he opened a manila folder for each student, holding their picture up to the camera and reciting the name of the historical event they'd be working on that quarter, so the class could get to know a bit about one another even though they were working independently.

"Greer Richmond..." Leipziger read Greer's name on the folder before opening it and reaching for the photo. He stopped for a split second before lifting it to the camera and smiling in a way that made me think he might have bodies buried in his basement. It reminded me of Eugenia. "...is researching the wreck of the *Jonathan Richmond* and its effect on Astoria, Oregon."

In the photo, Greer looked younger, but her long, pale hair was unmistakable. She was smiling, her creamy skin accented by makeup that made her eyes look dark and mysterious. Her teeth were white and straight. I wanted to run my tongue along her exposed collarbone.

"I hate that picture," she said, cringing. "My mother made me get these glamour shots in high school, and I didn't have any other pictures of myself to use."

"I think you look...beautiful, but serious. Like a news anchor on television."

She made a face.

"Thanks, but TV news isn't real news. It's entertainment. I'm going to be a newspaper reporter."

The video ended, and Greer pulled up the electronic family tree she'd been working on. One side was completely bare. She took a deep breath.

"My mother's side of the tree—Sterling's side—is a bit of a treasure trove. I followed clues that led me back to the Jonathan Richmond who came from England to Astoria and commissioned Richmond House in 1850. The house was completed in 1851."

"He's *the* Jonathan Richmond?" I asked, excited. "The ship was named after him?"

"No. According to Sterling, the ship was named after this JR's grandfather." She gestured to the other side of the screen. "And since we're working together, you might as well know that I don't really know anything about my father or how to contact him. It's a dead end. Let's just focus on the Richmond side."

"What if we just looked up his name and the fact that he used to live here at one point and start from there?"

Seconds passed before she spoke. "Yeah, that would be the place to start, only..."

"Only what?"

"Only, I don't know his name. I don't know who my father is. But I'm trying to find out."

"Sweetheart," I said, unsure of what else to say and surprised at how comfortably the affectionate nickname fell from my lips every chance I got. She was finally opening up to me, and I didn't want to spook her. "I'm so sorry."

"Don't be. I know he lived in Astoria, probably near Richmond House, when my mother was a teenager. They had access to each other. I'm going to find out who he is. It's part of the reason I'm here."

"Is there anything I can do to help?"

"Promise you'll still be my friend if I find out he's someone terrible?"

"Lucky for you, I've already cornered the market on terrible fathers," I replied, smiling. "Everything's going to be fine. You'll see."

12

GREER

Things were turning around. Slapping rain and vicious wind always seemed to be right around the corner, and I had a lot to unpack when it came to the bombshells Oren had dropped about my family, but nothing could pop the candy-colored bubble I'd been floating around in since I'd asked Jace if I could stay on the tarp and watch him work earlier this week.

Jace spent more and more time at Richmond House—even on weekends—working on the boats and doing yardwork for Sterling when it wasn't too wet. I knew I was acting desperate, showing up everywhere he was to keep him company, but he never made me feel like I was interrupting him or like he'd rather be alone. Jace had a unique view of the world, and our conversations revealed something new about him every day. He said he didn't have a favorite color, but when I pressed him, he said his favorite color was "sunset." His favorite food was beef jerky—he ate it every day. He liked country music and classic rock, knew a lot about history, and was a virtual encyclopedia when it came to anything that had moving parts.

I knew Jace was working today because I could see his

truck, but I couldn't find him anywhere. The past few days had been dry, and the tall golden grass in the field was now even taller and infused with green as the ground prepared to leave winter behind and embrace the new season. Armed with a brown-and-orange-plaid blanket better suited for a fall picnic, the paperback I'd been reading, and an apple I'd stolen from the kitchen when Eugenia wasn't looking, I decided to sit in the grass and read, Richmond House looming above and over me like the grand dame she was.

I folded the blanket into a seat cushion, unwilling to tamp down too much of the tall grass, and picked an inconspicuous spot in the corner of the field with a view that faced the back tree line and the partially hidden tool shed. Maybe Jace would spot me, and I could convince him to take a break with me.

Sitting down with my legs crossed like a butterfly, the grass hid me entirely from view. I bit into my apple and opened my book, enjoying the breeze that rippled through the grass and the faint sound of a motor running in the distance. A few minutes later, a small gap in the grass revealed Eugenia walking toward the shed. Just as I went to poke my head up and shout a greeting, a girl in an oversized green army jacket thrown over a white dress and tennis shoes emerged from the trees. I froze in shock before ducking down.

Eugenia's face contorted with anger. She gestured for the girl to go back into the woods the way she came, and when the girl lifted her face in defiance, I saw it wasn't a girl at all but a very petite young woman. I heard Eugenia say, "almost there." The unknown woman extended her hand toward the house, speaking to Eugenia rapidly. I thought I heard Jace's name before Eugenia slapped her hard across the face. My stomach dipped, shocked at the violence. The unknown woman rubbed her cheek, glaring at Eugenia before turning around and walking back into the woods.

Eugenia stood in place for several minutes, presumably to ensure the woman had gone, before trudging back to the house. I remembered the apple suspended in my hand and took a belated bite despite my churning stomach. Now I had even more questions about the inner workings of Richmond House. Who was that woman? Why was she visiting Eugenia secretly? The obvious answer was that the woman was Anna, Eugenia's daughter, but I didn't think so. Why would Eugenia slap her own daughter and send her away like that into the woods? Anna could have just come into the house to visit her mother. Even if what Oren told me was true, that my grandmother made Eugenia and Anna move out, there was never any talk of Eugenia losing her job or Anna being banned from the property. Besides, my grandmother was long dead. She died shortly after my mother left Richmond House.

I was suddenly tired, tired of trying to figure everything out on my own. Without bothering to spread the blanket out any farther, I set the apple aside and relaxed my body backward into the grass, letting it support my weight, and I closed my eyes. The humming motor in the distance was louder and wove its way in and out of my consciousness as I floated away, my face turned toward the sun.

I woke to a roar. Machinery. A shout. Then, silence.

I pushed up to a seated position and tried to orient myself, so I could figure out what had startled me awake. I stood up in the field and saw Jace swinging off a riding mower just feet from where I'd been dozing. Inches from where my hair had been splayed out, blending in with the top of the grass. Anger radiated off him as he approached, and not for the first time in my life, I wanted to turn and run in the other direction. I've never been hit before, never been in a physical fight, but the violence of Eugenia's slap was fresh in my mind. Jace walked toward me like he wanted to slap me across my face or shake me until my brain liquefied.

When he came within a few feet of me, he stopped. He said nothing; I watched his hands shake before he clenched his fists. There was no, "What the fuck, Greer?" No, "What the hell are you doing out here?" He just stood there in front of me, drowning me in the liquid black of his eyes. Then he looked down at his feet.

"Jace—" I started.

"Do you know how close you just came to dying, Greer?" he asked in a frighteningly soft voice. "Do you have any idea?"

Melodramatic much?

"Come on; I wasn't 'close to dying.' You saw me and stopped."

I didn't think it was possible, but he managed to look even more furious.

"What if I hadn't been paying attention? What if I'd been playing around with the radio or watching an eagle circling? Your fucking *brains* would be covering those blades right now. And guess what else? I'd be the one who'd have to take the mower apart and clean them off before putting it back together again."

"I'm sorry. I didn't know you were going to mow the field today, and I fell asleep. I saw Eugenia and—"

"I don't give a rat's ass about Eugenia. I don't understand how you could be so stupid. Were you hiding? Were you hiding from me? Is this some sort of joke?"

"What? No. I was just reading my book and eating my apple, and I fell asleep!"

Jace ran one hand through his hair, still shaking, fighting for composure.

He almost killed you. And it's tearing him up inside.

I knew it wasn't the time, that I should be downplaying the situation, reassuring him to assuage his anger, but the spike of adrenaline I'd experienced when I'd woken up was starting to wane, replaced by a torrent of emotions. I wasn't sure if I started crying because it finally hit me that I'd almost died or because Jace was so angry with me after our friendship had finally begun to flourish, but I welcomed the tears that flooded my eyes and dropped onto my cheeks. It felt good to fall apart. I let out a hoarse sob and wrapped my arms around myself in a practiced gesture.

My tears worked like a bucket of cold water to calm Jace's vitriol. In an instant, he'd stepped closer and wrapped his arms around me. Now I was the one shaking, having come close to death on this random morning in late March all because I was in the wrong place at the wrong time.

And because you were stupid.

"I'm so mad at you, sweetheart," Jace murmured to me as he continued to hold me. "So fucking mad. That could have ended so differently. I almost killed you, and I don't think I'd have been able to live with that."

A few moments of silence passed before I lifted my chin.

"Do you—do you want to talk?" I asked.

"I don't think I can right now. I can't believe you willingly chose to do something that fucking stupid."

"I'm sorry," I wailed, a fresh batch of tears streaming from my eyes.

Jace released me and went after the blanket, unfolding it and spreading it out into the field well away from where the mower was cooling down. He sat down heavily and waited while I found a spot. I drew my knees into my chest and wrapped my arms around them in a defensive pose.

"You wanted to talk?" His voice still sounded strained, like he was only just holding on to his sanity.

"I want you to know that I'm not playing a game. I just wanted to read in the field, and I fell asleep. I haven't been sleeping very well at night."

"You must be one helluva heavy sleeper."

"I guess I am."

I've learned to sleep through a lot of noises. My mother vomiting into the powder room toilet directly below my bedroom. Workout videos and the steady swishing of her elliptical machine in the wee hours of the morning.

I tapped a delicate pattern against the heel of my boot. Not-a-gain. Not-a-gain. Not-a-gain.

"I'm sorry if I overreacted, but I just—"

"You're angry because Sterling would have fired you—even if it was an accident."

"What? No. That's *not* why I'm mad, Greer. I'm not even mad, exactly. It just scared me to see you lying out there in the grass. I thought you'd...I don't know...accidently overdosed or something. And then when I realized...I cut the motor just in time. Everything happened so fast." He picked up a long blade of grass and began twisting it into a shape.

"Why would you think I'd overdosed?" I asked. "I don't even do drugs."

"I don't know."

"Jace."

"I know you're having some...family problems. In my experience, when women have problems, they try to take the edge off however they can."

"With drugs?"

"Drugs, alcohol, sex. When I saw you...on your back that way..." He took a deep breath. "It reminded me of Sheryll. My mother."

"I...I don't understand."

"She's overdosed a few times, and once I found her in the yard. Back then, she was on heroin. So, when I saw you, my brain made the connection. I thought you might already be dead."

"Oh my God," I said, unsure of what to say. "Is your mother okay now?"

"Depends on what you mean by 'okay.' She's alive. She's around."

"But you don't know where she is? She doesn't live with you and your dad?" Jace's lips thinned. I was asking too many questions, but I couldn't stop myself.

"She left him a long time ago. Left both of us."

"I'm so sorry, Jace."

"Don't be. Mothers are overrated."

His words hit me like a thunderclap in a way no slap ever could.

"God, Greer," he said. "I'm sorry. I wasn't thinking."

"It's okay." My voice sounded hollow even to my ears.

"No, it's not. I shouldn't have said that. Not to you."

Not to me?

My emotions, front and center since I woke to the sound of the motor near my head, swung to anger.

"You don't know me. You don't know anything about me. I'm not going to fall apart just because you think mothers are overrated."

"I didn't mean—"

"You know, I didn't have some perfect, happy childhood. My mother had issues too."

He gave me a level stare. "Your mom was on drugs?"

"No, but she—you remember how you thought I had an eating disorder?"

"It was your mom."

"Yeah. She was anorexic."

"Was it...bad?"

107

"Bad enough that it killed her."

"I didn't realize you could die from an eating disorder," he said slowly. "She starved to death?"

"More like the lack of nutrients caused her heart to fail."

He was quiet for a moment. He gestured for me to give him my hand, and when I did, he set a perfectly formed flower, made from a single blade of grass, into my palm. I smiled.

"Impressive," I said.

"Thank you for telling me about your mom. Do they—do you know what caused it? The eating disorder?"

Now I was at a crossroads. I wanted to tell him what Oren had told me about my grandfather, but I wasn't sure I could trust him. Jace worked for Sterling, and if he told him I'd been dredging up past family scandals, Sterling might ask me to leave before I found out the truth—about everything. But I craved the comfort of having someone to talk things through with. In the end, I couldn't resist.

"A few days ago, before I found you on the tarp, I ran into Oren, and I asked him about those rumors you mentioned."

I expected Jace to try to distance himself from the fact that he was the one who told me about Anna's suspected parentage, but he just sat back and nodded.

"Anyway," I said. "Oren said Sterling lavished my mother with attention from the time she was born until shortly before Anna was born thirteen years later. Then, when Anna was born, Sterling began ignoring my mother and bonded the same way with Anna."

"So, he dropped your mom right when she hit puberty."

"Yes, and Oren also said my mother did everything she could to get his attention, to be the kind of person she thought he wanted."

We both sat for a moment, suddenly aware of the implications of what I was really saying. "She wanted to be thinner," I continued. "Smaller. More like a girl, less like a woman. Because...that's what he liked? That's what he wanted?"

"Sick fuck," Jace said. "His own daughter? And Anna might be his daughter too?"

"We don't know for sure. We don't know anything for sure. Oren said my mother told my grandmother about Sterling and Eugenia when Anna was little, and then my grandmother made them move out. My mother left days later. She was already pregnant with me."

"Did Sterling kick her out?"

"He didn't kick her out. She ran away, and he tried to keep in touch with her. At least for a while. But why would he bother when he didn't care about her anymore?"

"Maybe it was less about her and more about you."

"Maybe. But he's just as indifferent toward me. He didn't even want me to come here. Not really."

It didn't add up. The pieces of the puzzle were starting to appear, but they wouldn't come together in my mind. Not yet anyway.

13
JACE

Greer was still pretty shaken up when I left her on the steps outside the back door of Richmond House. I didn't want to go, didn't want to leave her there with a man I suspected of having a thing for his own prepubescent daughters, but she was right; at this point, it was just a theory. And even if it was true, all of it, Sterling was no danger to her now. She was a fully grown woman, tall and curvy and beautiful. The only threat was Sterling finding out she knew anything at all about his secret. If it was true, there wasn't much she could do—any sexual abuse of her mother or Anna happened in the eighties and nineties, well past Oregon's statute of limitations—but Sterling could retaliate in other ways, I'd imagine.

She had handed me her computer before I left. Our shared truths and resulting revelations had left her feeling sick, but she needed to check her email daily for class assignments and feedback. I told her I'd head down to the library and continue researching what had already been written on the *Jonathan Richmond*. I liked doing the research, carefully jotting down complete passages of text and logging the various books and periodicals I'd pulled the information from. I'd discovered a talent for organizing—my color-coded accordion folder of various notes, sources, and photocopied images was a source of pride. I was anxious to get back at it, lose myself in the world of a long-ago voyage gone awry, but I had a stop to make first.

I rapped my knuckles hard against the flimsy trailer door—no answer. I knocked again, louder. Finally, Linus jerked the door open. He was a big guy, dressed in just his boxers, his feet shoved into a pair of house shoes. I looked past him into the living room, where a topless middle-aged woman I didn't recognize from the trailer park sat drinking Bud Light from a bottle on a brown corduroy couch that had seen better days. Empty bottles and an overflowing ashtray littered the table in front of the couch.

"Who's your friend, Ly-Ly?" she slurred.

Linus quickly closed the door behind him and stepped out onto the porch.

"What's up, man? I'm busy."

"Yeah, I can tell."

"You want in on this? She's seriously loaded."

I couldn't be mad at him for asking. In the past, we'd shared plenty of married women willing to pay for the thrill of slumming it with a couple of well-endowed park boys—but the thought of walking in there now and pretending to want that woman made me sick.

"Nah, man. I got a girl."

"Oh, for real? My bad. Who is she?"

She's none of your fucking business.

Linus and I were the same age, though I'd made it a few years more than he had in school. We were both big guys, and he had a good-looking face I didn't want anywhere near Greer.

What the fuck was happening to me? First, I lost my

shit when I thought Greer was high, when I'd almost run her over with the mower. Then I told her all that ancient history about my mom. Now I was turning down great money for a half hour's worth of work, tops, money that could help me get out of this damn cesspool of depravity, and telling Linus that I wasn't single anymore? I couldn't believe it, but it had happened. In my mind, Greer Richmond was my girl. She was vulnerable, like my mom. But unlike my mom, I could do something about it. I could protect her.

"Just someone I met at Old Man Richmond's. Speaking of, I need a favor."

"What?" Linus asked suspiciously. In our world, favors weren't handed out like candy from a parade float. They were earned. Or paid for. "You still got that...friend? In the Department?"

"Yeah..." Linus drew out his answer.

"I want to see Sterling Richmond's criminal record."

"How am I supposed to get that?"

"I don't know—just ask for it. I'll grease some palms if necessary."

He sighed, looking back toward the door. "Okay, man, I'll ask, but if I can get it for you, the palm you're going to be greasing is mine."

"That sounds fucking gross when you say it like that."

Linus laughed. "I'll be in touch." With that, he pushed the door open and backed up into his trailer ass first, slamming the door closed.

I did a quick check of my own trailer across the road before heading out. I only went there to eat dinner and sleep—everything was still locked up tight. I'd splurged on the lock—it protected everything I had in the world. I protected my future.

I found an empty table at the library and fired up

Greer's computer before entering the password she gave me—04141993. Her birthday, coming up soon. She had an email waiting from her professor. I scanned it, noting its flirty tone that bordered on inappropriate, but it wasn't urgent and didn't require a response. I switched from Greer's email application to a spreadsheet we'd created listing potential sources on the wreck. It was a lot higher tech than my file folder, but I didn't have a computer. Even if I did, I'd probably still use the folder. I liked having things in front of me, holding them in my hands. How else could you make sure something was real?

I started at the top, cross-checking whether the listed resource was available at this library, another library in the area, or whether we could purchase it somewhere. An hour flew by like minutes before I noticed a person standing to the side of the desk. It'd been years, so it took me a few beats to recognize her.

"Hi, Jace."

"Anna. Hi."

"I saw you over here, and I decided to come over and say hello."

"I'm glad you did. What are you up to these days?"

Anna had always been a slight girl, but looking at her now was difficult, knowing what I thought I knew. She wore a thin, billowy white dress that touched her ankles and was better suited for the summer months. Her arms emerged from the sleeves like sticks, and her face appeared small and childlike. Her hair, somewhere between brown and blonde, was scraped back from her face into a severe bun, drawing attention to her thin features. "Nothing much," she answered. "I work at the bookstore down the street. The library buys books from us sometimes, so I was just dropping off a few new titles. What are you doing here?"

"I'm just...working on a research project. For a friend."

Anna's already thin lips seemed to tighten into a frown, reminding me of Eugenia when she was particularly annoyed and had to drop her fake-ass smile.

"Listen, Jace...I don't know when or if I'll see you again..."

Okay...

"And I've always had a bit of a crush on you. I'm not ashamed to admit it. I think we have a lot in common, and I was wondering if you'd like to...take me out sometime."

I admired her confidence. I remembered her because our school was so small, but I'd never thought of her in that way, never considered her girlfriend material. One, I didn't have girlfriends. And two, she wasn't my type.

Because Greer is your type—tall, shapely, beautiful. Smart. Nervous. Alone.

"Look, Anna, I'm flattered. I just—"

"Also, you should know you're the most handsome man I've ever seen in real life. I've been watching you since grade school, and I just know we could be so good together. So don't say 'no.' Don't say anything. Just think about it."

Psycho alert!

Even if I wasn't wholly, unexpectedly obsessed with Greer Richmond, I wouldn't touch Anna with a ten-foot pole. I had just about all the crazy I could take in my life living with Jesse.

"Anna, I'm seeing someone," I said, trying to swerve the conversation.

"What?" What little color was there drained from her face. "I know you don't have a girlfriend. Who is she?"

She said the last sentence so forcefully I wasn't sure I wanted to reveal Greer's name. "It's not really official yet. I mean, I haven't really talked to her about the whole boyfriend-girlfriend thing, so I'd rather not say."

"What is there to talk about? What kind of girl wouldn't want to be with you?"

"That's so nice of you to say, Anna. Anyway, I need to get going."

"The research project for your 'friend'—are you helping her? Your girlfriend?"

I let out a heavy sigh. "Yeah."

"So, it's Greer Richmond then. My mother told me she's working on a project for school."

"Like I said, I haven't talked with her about it, so I'd appreciate it if—"

"Oh, I won't say anything. I'm not allowed to talk to Greer, and I doubt she'd get off her high horse long enough to give me the time of day."

Not allowed?

"I don't think that's true, Anna. Greer's not like that."

"Jace...Greer might be the resident Richmond princess right now. But she won't be forever. My mother and I... things are in motion. Someday soon, everything will be different. So, if you're interested in being the master of Richmond House, you're betting on the wrong Richmond."

The fuck?

"I'm not—"

She turned and practically bolted from my sight before I could say another word.

14

GREER

I reluctantly sat behind the steering wheel of the Bronco, tapping out my anxiety on the wheel. At least it wasn't raining. Interacting with Sterling as if nothing was wrong, despite my suspicions, was a daily struggle. My nerves were at an all-time high. I should leave. I knew that. If I truly believed Sterling had abused my mother, I'd want nothing to do with him or this place. But I had unfinished business here. Finding my father. Jace. And maybe finding a way to deliver some justice.

Tap, tap, tap, pause.

Tap, tap, tap, pause.

I'd been practicing my driving with Jace in the parking lot of the library and on a few of Astoria's deserted side streets, and he thought I was ready for a longer trip. He exaggerated the buckling of his seatbelt, checking to make sure it was fastened securely and the strap was snug, trying to make me laugh. It worked. This came after he'd insisted on buckling *my* seatbelt for me, looking into my eyes as he used his big hand to click it into place and adjust the strap between my breasts. He smelled faintly of cloves, and his bare forearms were corded with muscles.

Tension—sexual and otherwise—permeated the cab.

"Relax, sweetheart. It's just a beat-up old truck. Your only job is to turn the wheel so that it stays on the road."

"But all the turns and—"

"Don't worry about that. No one even comes up here besides Sterling, Eugenia, and Oren. And me. We can go as slow as we need to. Now put the key into the ignition and turn it on."

I did as he said, the Bronco roaring to life. I winced.

I pressed the brake, and Jace guided my hand onto the gear shift, putting the car in drive. His hand felt warm and smooth over mine, and I was suddenly hyperaware of the weight of it and how easy it would be for me to turn my hand palm-up and intertwine my slender fingers with his long, tan ones.

"Now, very slowly, put your foot on the brake..."

I pressed my foot onto the gas instead and flooded the engine.

"Jesus, baby, the brake! The brake, not the gas!"

"I'm sorry!"

I wish I could say the drive to the library went off without a hitch and that I was a natural, but I'd be lying. It took almost forty-five minutes. The worst part was navigating the road from Richmond House to the two-lane highway that took us into town. I came to a complete stop at the beginning of every hairpin turn and made Jace get out to check that no car was coming.

By the time I pulled into the parking lot of the library, I was a mess. My hands were shaking, and my heart hadn't stopped pounding since a particularly slow turn elicited a blaring honk from the irritated driver behind us.

I put the Bronco in park, turned it off, and was out of the car before Jace had the chance to say anything. Leaning back against the driver's side door, I tried to calm down while waiting for him to pull the keys out of the ignition and come around to me.

When he did, instead of saying anything at all, he put his arms around me. I broke down, sobbing against his chest in a public parking lot in full view of anyone and everyone going in and out of the library. I was such a baby.

"It's okay, sweetheart," he crooned, his arms blocking out the world around us. "You don't have to do it again until you're ready. I'm sorry I pushed you."

I sniffed and looked up at him with tear-soaked eyes. I didn't say anything, just watched his dark eyes, full of concern, stare back at me. I wanted him to kiss me. I wanted him to take off his shirt so I could rest my cheek against his warm skin. At that moment, I would have given anything for him to just absorb me whole.

I lifted onto my toes and tilted my chin up to his mouth, my need unmistakable. Jace shook his head.

"Jesus Christ, Greer. Not right now. Not like this. You're shaking."

Stung by the rejection, I lowered back down and counted to three, again and again, keeping my eyes straight ahead of me on his shirt. Eventually, he took his arms from around me.

"I think we should go inside now," I said, my voice sounding high and strained.

"Greer—"

"It's fine. Forget about it. I'm not a good driver. It stresses me out, and I'm worried about finishing this research. Will you help me?"

He waited a long moment, weighing my words.

"Okay," he said finally.

An enclosed fishbowl of a room hidden along the library's back wall was most often used for meetings and other community events, but it also housed the library's collection of maritime historical documents. Being that Astoria was a town built on the maritime industry and also the oldest Euro-settlement on the north Pacific Coast, there was quite a collection on display.

Using the spreadsheet Jace had previously cross-checked against available materials, we pulled what we could from the shelves before settling in. Jace sat down in one of the chairs circling a table set up in the middle of the room. Leaning back, he put his feet up on the table next to the stack of reference texts in front of him and locked his hands behind his head, trying to gauge my mood after what happened outside.

I took off my navy wool blazer and draped it over the back of the chair before sitting down beside him. I adjusted the waistband of my jeans and the pink silk blouse I wore and tucked my long hair behind my ears before opening the text and my notepad to transcribe notes. I lifted my chin and looked at him. I was shaken by the drive, embarrassed by his rejection—but also suddenly determined. The tightening of Jace's jaw, the look in his eyes...he'd wanted to kiss me too. I was sure of it. For the first time in my life, I wanted to use everything I had going for me to convince him he should.

But now, Jace was all business. He started with a summary.

"So, John Jacob Astor came in 1811 and founded Astoria as a fur-trading outpost. We went to war with the Brits the next year. Astor *sold* Astoria to them rather than lose it during the war, and the city became known as Fort George," he recited from memory.

"Then in 1818, England established joint ownership with the Oregon Territory before abandoning it in 1846," I finished, though I had to consult my notes for the exact dates.

"When did your family set up shop here?"

"Jonathan Richmond moved the family from England to Astoria. He built Richmond House in 1851 and died in"—I flipped back a few pages in my notebook to check—"1870. So, he got to live in the house for almost twenty years."

"What year was Sterling born?"

"1935. Three generations separate them."

"Let's skip ahead and read specifically about Pacific Coast shipwrecks," Jace said excitedly, pulling out an illustrated book on the subject from his pile. We huddled together and searched for the *Jonathan Richmond*, but it wasn't listed in the Table of Contents.

A knock sounded on the door.

"Come in," I called.

Heidi, the head librarian, pushed open the door, looking very much the quintessential "librarian" in her cardigan and glasses.

"Hello, you two. Saw you were in here, at it again, and I wanted to let you know that I took the liberty of ordering a copy of one of the books you were looking for but couldn't find. We should have had it all along—I don't know where it went off to."

"That's so nice of you," I gushed. "We just hit sort of a dead end."

"Well, I have to warn you, dear...I read through a few of the meatier chapters last night, and...the research...the author...it all paints a rather unflattering picture of your ancestors."

I practically snatched the book out of her hand. "In what sense, exactly?"

"Just remember...history is subjective. Sometimes it's in the eye of the beholder."

"She knows what 'subjective' means," Jace piped up.

121

"I'm just saying," Heidi continued unfazed, "just because you read it in a book doesn't mean it's true."

I tucked the book into my backpack. "Thanks, Heidi. I'll look through it tonight at home."

"You're very welcome." She retreated the way she came and shut the door.

"That was interesting," Jace said. "Want me to take it and look at it for you?"

"No, I need something to do at night in that big, old house. Avoiding Sterling is easy, but I'm just...I get nervous there all by myself with nothing to do. Maybe I could come over to your place? Just to hang out?"

He shook his head. "Sorry, sweetheart. That's not going to happen. It's not a very nice place."

"What do you mean? You live there, so it can't be that bad."

He sighed. Once again, I could tell he was choosing his words carefully. "Do you know what a trailer park is?"

"Of course. There are actually some very nice ones...I've heard."

"Well, I grew up in a trailer park. And there was nothing nice about it. Is nothing nice. I don't want you there."

"But if I already know it's a trailer park, and it's not the nicest, why won't you let me come over?"

"Because knowing something and seeing it with your own eyes are two different things. I don't want anything getting in the way of...whatever we have going on here. Especially because I'm not that guy. I'm not a trailer park guy. I don't...I don't want you thinking of me that way. Pretty soon, I'll have a regular apartment, and you can visit me there. Hell, you can move in if you want."

Move in with him? Was he serious—or was he just being hyperbolic? I smiled, thinking about how just a month ago he was going out of his way to ignore me.

I decided to change the subject. "Are you coming over tomorrow?"

"Yeah, but it's supposed to rain, and I have to get some work in for Sterling. On Saturday, though, we should visit the wreckage."

"The wreckage of the *Jonathan Richmond*? Isn't it buried?"

"Only during the winter months when the wind blows sand onto the beach. If we get up and go when the tide's out, we should be able to see it. And if we go early enough, we'll have the place to ourselves. I can pick you up on Saturday first thing."

"It's a date, then." I held his gaze with my own, daring him to contradict me until he was the one who finally looked away.

"Yeah," he said, running his fingers through the long, dark hair on the top of his head and exhaling loudly in surrender. "It's whatever you want it to be, sweetheart. I'm done fighting you."

15
JACE

My alarm went off at five thirty, but I was already awake. I jumped in the shower, slicked back my hair, and changed into jeans and a black T-shirt. I grabbed my peacoat, the only coat I owned, and headed out. I pulled up to Richmond House twenty-two minutes later. Greer sat on the porch steps in the waning darkness.

God, she was a stunner. Her hair was down around her face, damp from the mist coming off the river and curling up at the ends. She was wearing her white, quilted coat. She'd cinched it over her jeans and those red rubber boots.

When she saw me pull up, she started walking around the field to where the Bronco was idling.

"Hi," she said breathlessly, her cheeks rosy in the dawn cold.

"Hi, yourself," I said. I wished I could pull her face to mine and kiss her. Instead, I just stared at her. I'm such a fucking idiot.

"How did you sleep?"

"Great."

Terribly.

Restlessly.

Trapped in an endless cycle of filthy thoughts about you.

"How did you sleep?" I asked her, enjoying the absurdity of it. I don't think I'd ever asked anyone how they'd slept in my entire life before Greer.

The pink in her cheeks deepened as she looked away.

"Okay, I guess. It took me a while to get to sleep, but once I...found a way to relax...I slept well."

Found a way to relax? Fuck. Me.

Had my little Greer touched herself while thinking about me? Yeah, she'd made herself come gasping my name. I'd bet money on it. She'd wanted to tell me without telling me; that's why she can't make eye contact right now. Rock-hard in my jeans at the thought, I took the highway back toward town, the world beginning to lighten around us in incremental degrees. We hadn't done anything sexual yet. We hadn't kissed. We hadn't even acknowledged that... whatever "this" was between us was a real relationship. I still wasn't sure what she expected of me, but the air in the cab was thick with anticipation.

I hung a right on Commercial Street in the direction of Jetty Sands, the beach that held the remains of the *Jonathan Richmond*. All the way down the street, Greer's face was pushed to the window. She watched as shop owners arrived at their places of business, prepared to open despite the lack of tourists in early April. She smiled as we passed a charming coffee shop located in an old cannery building, the only place actually open. Warm air billowed out the doors every time someone walked in or out, creating a shroud of steam when it hit the chilly morning air outside.

"Want to go in?" I asked.

"Do we have time? What about the tide?"

"We have time."

I parked underneath the bridge near the Maritime

Memorial, and we went in together, enjoying the warmth on our faces as we stepped inside.

"What can I get you?" asked the woman behind the counter. She had bright purple hair and a lip piercing and was making eye contact with me in a way that had me thinking that if I asked her to step into the back room of the shop, she'd happily oblige. But I wasn't feeling it. Obviously, because I wouldn't be able to explain it to Greer, but also because I couldn't imagine putting my hands on that woman when I had the opportunity to spend the morning with the one I couldn't stop thinking about. The only woman I could ever remember wanting.

Instinctually, Greer took a step closer to me, angling her body in front of mine so that her hip grazed my groin. I cleared my throat.

"Ladies first," I said to Greer.

"I'll have a nonfat peppermint latte, please," she said primly.

"And a black coffee," I echoed.

Purple hair stepped away to make Greer's latte, and I couldn't resist teasing her.

"Peppermint, huh? I didn't realize the holiday season extended to April."

"Well, now you know. I like peppermint. Peppermint and lemon are my two favorite flavors."

She smiled up at me, and I suddenly knew what my favorite flavor would be. Her. Her mouth. Her skin. Her—

"That will be $6.25."

I pulled out my wallet and handed over a five and two ones.

"Keep the change."

Greer and I grabbed our drinks and left, the cold, salty air hitting our exposed skin. In the distance, I could hear the bark of the sea lions from the pier they'd taken over.

Neither of us attempted conversation again once we were back in the car, but it wasn't uncomfortable. It was companionable. By the time we pulled up to the beach, it was light outside.

Greer turned, looking at me like she wanted to tell me something but unsure of how to broach the subject. She apparently decided against saying anything, turning back toward the door and getting out of the cab. I followed.

I led her onto the deserted beach. Seagulls swirled above us while the sandpipers chased the waves rushing to the shore. In the distance, toward the waterline, sat an irregularly shaped mound of sand. Bingo.

I wrapped an arm around her, and together we strolled the beach toward the wreckage buried in the sand. She had no idea, scanning the beach for what she assumed would be a giant, abandoned ship.

"This is it?" she said, raising her voice to be heard over the roar of the waves as we approached the wreck.

"Hey, this is a very famous wreck."

"I don't know why…it just looks like a pile of sand."

I slowly led her around to the other side. There, the *Jonathan Richmond's* iron skeleton sat partially exposed, as firmly anchored as it had been ever since it'd run ashore more than a hundred fifty years ago. Greer's eyes widened as she took in the rusty, truncated remains of the massive ship, reduced over time to just a dozen or so vertical support ribs that evenly lined the frame. Inside the skeleton was nothing but sand—a wall of it on the opposite side and a carpet beneath. She stepped between the beams that lined the wreck like rib bones in a whale skeleton—slipping a notebook out of the pocket of her coat. Touching a barely recognizable, barnacle-covered bolt up high on one of the iron ribs, she began to speak.

"I read through that book Heidi gave us, and I found

out...some things," she said, sounding anxious. "About the *Jonathan Richmond*. But I couldn't confirm anything conclusive beyond the company, the date of the wreck, and the captain's name."

"We knew in the beginning that might be all we're able to get. Maybe there just isn't much to find."

She flipped through her notebook.

"The ship was commissioned and owned by J. Richmond & Reeves of Brighton, England. No idea when it was built."

She stopped, stalling. I realized there was something she didn't want to tell me.

"Go on," I said. "What else did you find out?"

She took a deep breath and blew it out.

"Jonathan Richmond—the one who built Richmond House—this book accuses him of making his fortune in the slave trade. There's no actual evidence on record as far as I can tell, but the historian who wrote the book Heidi gave us...he wrote that Richmond was a ne'er-do-well sailor who shunned the family business in England, only to turn around and revive it in Astoria when he inherited his grandfather's original ship, the *Jonathan Richmond*. This... historian hypothesized that Richmond wanted into the business of transporting slaves and chose Astoria because it was a new and virtually untapped port to pass them through at that time. The *Jonathan Richmond* was big and fast, easily making a half dozen...runs...that first year, and that's how Richmond financed his fleet and the house so quickly. It's how he made the fortune Sterling enjoys today. The book says that on its final voyage, the *Jonathan Richmond*, Richmond's largest and fastest ship, set sail under Captain William Reid from Guinea, West Africa loaded with"—she consulted her notes—"1,500 pounds of ballast and thirty passengers on March 15, 1859. It's said to have wrecked on a sandy spit at the mouth of the Columbia River on October fourteenth of that same year. All aboard were found shot in the head, including twenty-two West Africans headed for a life of slavery in the Pacific Northwest."

Greer choked out the rest of her notes, her eyes downcast.

"If it's true, I can't believe I didn't know this. Do you think Sterling knows? Oren?"

"I don't know," I said truthfully. "Maybe not. Sometimes people go to great lengths to rewrite history in their favor. And like you said, it might not even be true. It's not common knowledge, or we would have found it in the library's archive. It's just one historian's obscure research and opinion."

Greer turned away to look out over the ocean. With the wreckage in the foreground, she looked like she belonged there. Like she was a mermaid who'd spent the past hundred years guarding this wreck. I had to touch her. I knew it was wrong, but I couldn't help myself. I wrapped my arms around her from behind, enjoying the way she felt in my arms. She was tall, but I was much taller. And she was so fine-boned that I felt like I was handling glass. That's how I always felt around Greer. Like I was big and dark and violent, and she was light and fragile. That if I touched her, she'd shatter in my hands. It didn't stop me from unzipping the length of her coat. I pushed my hands underneath her sweater and rested my hands on the skin above her jeans. I wanted to explore further. God, I wanted to touch more of her skin, but I told myself I wasn't in a hurry. My hands were on her warm, velvet skin. It was enough.

Her hands came to rest over mine, where they were anchored around her slim waist. We stood there for a few minutes, watching the seagulls swoop down into the sea before pulling back up and circling overhead. Greer began tapping on my hands. At first, I thought she was trying to tell me something, spell something out, but as she sighed, I realized she didn't know she was doing it. It wasn't long before I found the pattern.

One, two, three, pause. One, two, three, pause.

"Why do you do that?" I said into her ear. My voice sounded deep with the arousal that was again thickening beneath my jeans now that she'd pressed her ass against me. Greer might be small-boned and slim, but her full breasts and soft ass, hidden underneath sweaters and heavy coats this past month, confirmed that I was holding a woman in my arms.

"Do what?" she asked breathlessly, obviously enjoying the feel of me from behind and my hands on her body.

"Tap things. In a pattern. In threes. I've seen you do it before."

She froze, and seconds passed in silence before she wrenched away from me.

"I don't know what you're talking about." She turned to face me, the sides of her coat flapping in the wind. "The tide's coming in. I think it's time you take me home."

What the fuck?

What just happened? One minute I had my hands on her and was pressed against her delectable ass, and the next minute she wanted to go home? Her eyes darted around, looking anywhere but at my face.

"Greer." One word. Delivered with shocking menace. "Explain to me what the fuck just happened."

"There's nothing to explain. Nothing happened. I just want to go home."

"Everything was fine until I asked you about your...the pattern." I was careful with my words.

"Well, I don't want to talk about it." She stood up straight, hands at her sides, and pushed her nose into the air. Greer wasn't stuck-up in the least, but she sure looked the part now. With her high cheekbones and her hair whipping wildly around us, she looked at me like I was beneath her. Exactly like she was the heir to a hundred-plus-year-old shipping empire, and I was the hired help.

Fuck that.

"You don't want to talk about it? Good, because that's not what I want to talk about either. Do you know what I want to talk about?"

She glared at me mutinously.

"Trick question, sweetheart. I don't want to talk anymore."

I grabbed her arm and jerked her to me, deliberately trying to scare her. I looked down at her face. If she turned her head or tried to shake me off, I'd let go. I'd take her home. But she didn't. Instead, she lifted her chin and stared into my eyes defiantly, daring me to kiss her.

I watched the blush creep up her neck and into her cheeks the longer I stared down at her. I lifted my hand and used my long, thick finger to trace her lips. How dare they be that perfect petal-pink color. How dare they be that full. That soft. Greer darted her tongue out to lick the tip of my finger. The wind hit the spot of moisture sending a cold frisson down my spine.

Oh, sweetheart.

Still in control, I replaced my finger with my lips. Greer was tall enough that I didn't have to double over to reach her. I sealed my lips over hers purposefully, creating pressure and contact but holding back, coaxing her to make the next move. She opened her mouth instinctively, and I slid my tongue inside. She released a sound of pent-up pleasure, of relief, that originated in the back of her throat, and I abandoned what I'd been trying to do—punish her for being so beautiful. Make her want me, and then reject her the way I'd felt rejected moments ago. Because it felt too good.

I moved my mouth to her neck, trailing my tongue along the underside of her jaw, then down toward her shoulder while she hummed, spurring me on. When I got to the place where her neck met her shoulder, I bit down, and she gasped, her fingers clutching my forearms. Her nipples, already pronounced under her thin sweater from the cold and her initial arousal, became shards scraping against my chest.

This is what I liked. What I needed. I was still at her neck, holding her to me like I was an apex predator, and she was my prey. I found her. I stalked her. I seduced her. Now she was mine to eat.

Returning to her lips, I kissed her using long, languorous strokes of my tongue, desperately wanting to make this the best kiss she'd ever have, trying to ruin her for anyone else. My hands returned to their previous position under her sweater, moving back and forth over the skin of her navel before climbing toward the undersides of her breasts. I held the weight of them in my hands before running my thumbs over her pointed nipples through the material of her bra. Just as I was contemplating breaking off our kiss so I could expose them and close my mouth over the melted-sugar tips, she reached for my belt, fumbling one-handed with the buckle.

She might as well have doused me in a bucket of ice water.

What the fuck was I doing, standing on a public beach, my hands on Greer Richmond's chest, mauling her?

I forced myself to remove my hands from underneath her sweater and took a step back.

"Jace?" Her voice was raspy and sexy as hell.

"We're not doing this." Once again, I sounded harsher than I intended, my breath pushing out in short pants.

"Not doing what?"

"This."

I turned to leave, walking as briskly as the sand would allow toward the car. I couldn't hear her behind me. I hoped she followed so I wouldn't have to go back out and look for her.

When I unlocked the Bronco, I looked over and could see her approaching in the distance, coat zipped and belted, arms wrapped around herself in a defensive position. God, I was such a dick. I wanted her so badly, but I didn't deserve her. Couldn't have her even if I did.

I cranked the heat inside the cab and waited for her to get in, rubbing my hands together against the chill of the wind.

She opened the passenger-side door; it squealed loudly as it extended and again as she pulled it shut behind her. For a moment, neither of us said anything. I used the passing moments to tick off all the reasons in my head that it would never work with Greer.

She was too young. I'm six years older, and I'd seen and done things she'd never understand.

She was too vulnerable. She'd lost her mother, her grandpa might be a pedophile, she just found out her family likely built their legacy on the backs of African slaves—she had too much going on right now to know what she wanted.

She was too innocent. I'd always have to keep myself in check around her, so I wouldn't scare her.

If Sterling found out, I'm pretty sure he'd fire me, and I wasn't sure I had enough saved up to change my life the way I wanted to. And if I didn't change my life, I'd never be worthy of someone like Greer.

And she'd leave me anyway, once she saw what I was, where I came from.

Holding all those reasons in my head, I turned to her, grasping to find the words to explain myself, but she beat me to it.

"I know I'm not very experienced in these things...being with someone, I mean...but I want to be with you. I want... you. I want you, Jace."

She stared at me, her brown eyes big and damp from the wind. With that, all my previous reasoning vanished. It didn't matter that she was young and vulnerable and naive. That I'd break her. That she'd break me. That she deserved better. Nothing mattered anymore when she looked at me like that.

"I want you too, sweetheart."

It was a bad idea. But it was already too late.

16

GREER

He drove me home. Just like on the ride to the beach, everything unspoken took precedence over actual words. Despite our mutual declarations, I didn't know what to expect moving forward. Jace seemed tense, almost angry. When he pulled up to Richmond House, it was clear he had no intention of getting out of the truck.

I felt sick over the possibility that my family made its fortune in the slave trade, but just like when I'd told Jace about the conversation I'd had with Oren about my mother, confessing the possibility had been cathartic in a way I hadn't anticipated.

I knew I could talk to Jace about anything, but I drew the line at talking about the anxious thoughts I couldn't control anymore. I just didn't want anyone to know. Not him, not anyone else. It was crazy, my superstitions and how I believed I could ward off evil with the power of three. It hadn't crept back into my life so much as it had never left, but I was confident I could get everything back on track, regain control, without anyone's help.

"I'll be back tomorrow," he said, drawing me away from my thoughts. "We're going on a drive. Be ready for me."

I slid out of the truck, and he barely waited for the door to close behind me before he backed up and peeled down the dirt tracks toward the road. I used the back door and entered the house, running right into Eugenia.

"Goodness! Welcome home, darling. Oren has come by, and we're all to have dinner together tonight. Won't that be lovely?"

It was good news. I'd have to endure Sterling's company, but I was anxious to get Oren alone and ask him about what I'd discovered.

"You'll want to change before dinner, of course, dear. It's formal dress."

Eugenia had already dressed for dinner in a long-sleeved jersey Pucci dress swirled in black, white, and pink and protected by a white apron, a dress that might have been hanging in her closet since the Italian designer's heyday. If she was already here and dressed, overseeing the kitchen prep, tonight's dinner must be special indeed.

I took the stairs two at a time up to my bedroom. It was only a little past nine in the morning—Jace had picked me up at dawn. It felt like days. I should take a nap, but I felt restless. Energized. I thought of Jace's big hands cupping me under my sweater, and I trembled with excitement. I'd take a bath, I decided. It might help me rest.

I gathered my toiletries into the little caddy Eugenia had supplied the day after I'd arrived and stepped out into the empty hallway. Walking toward the bathroom door, I heard the familiar squeal of pressure on a wooden floorboard sound above my head. I stopped and looked up. Seconds passed before a series of squeals moved away from me across the ceiling. Footsteps from above. Footsteps from the attic.

Sterling had expressly forbidden me from going up into the attic. But wouldn't he want to know if someone—or something—was playing around up there? It wasn't Eugenia—she was down in the kitchen. It could be Sterling himself, but the footsteps had sounded light. Almost playful. I turned around and walked in the opposite direction, away from the bathroom and toward the metal spiral stairs at the other end of the hallway that swirled from the ground floor to the attic.

When I got there, I set the caddy down in the hallway and took a tentative step off the second-floor landing and onto the stairs. I stood—hands on the rails—and looked down. I could see all the way to the butler's pantry below, where the stairs originated. If I fell, I'd die. Or at least be paralyzed. This open-concept thing really wasn't safe at all. Looking up, I saw a shadowy platform where the stairs stopped and the third-floor attic began.

I started to climb. I was still in the flat rubber boots I'd worn to the beach. The staircase itself didn't sway or rattle, but my boots let out a subtle squeak every time I climbed a step. Whoever was up there could hear me coming—no doubt about it. Almost to the top, my head popped above the second floor, and I got my first glimpse at the attic. I looked around as I came to rest on the top step.

I couldn't see anyone. The space was vast. And cold. While the floors below were divided into rooms with rugs, and lamps, and furniture, this space had no such niceties. It was just one open space that spanned the entire length and width of Richmond House. In the corner closest to me, I saw neat boxes stacked and labeled. Summer clothing. Christmas decorations. I stepped off the top step and farther into the space.

Trespassing through a maze of antique furniture, I marveled at the number of old-fashioned trunks stacked throughout the space, covered in a coating of dust so thick, it looked like gray paint. What was in them? To whom did they belong? By the look of them, they could be as old as the house itself, and my fingers itched to pop a few latches and dig through. But that would have to wait. What I thought I saw in the distance, stark white and easily visible even in the dim light, pulled me like a beacon.

Carefully, in case Sterling's warning about termite-infested wood turned out to be accurate, I covered the remaining yardage to reach the far side of the third floor, the portion of the attic directly above my bedroom. And Sterling's. In one corner sat a brass-framed twin bed, angled out from the wall and into the space. The comforter was white and covered with ruffles. Approaching the bed, I saw it was clean, without a speck of dust. Big, fluffy pink pillows dominated a headboard made of cream-colored linen and festooned with delicate pink ribbon bows spaced uniformly across. This was the bed of a little girl, one who loved ruffles and all things pink. But how could it be so clean?

I approached the opposite corner and couldn't make sense of what I saw. Running in rows from the wall to the middle of the attic space were what looked like...beds? Some sort of barracks? There were no mattresses, only open wooden frames with a thin, flat slab of plywood over the top, each connected to the one beside. I did some quick math—there were more than a hundred frames in the space.

A shout of laughter drifted up from the main-floor kitchen through the staircase opening on the other side of the house, and I reminded myself that I might not be alone up here. What had caused the creaks I'd heard earlier? I thought I'd heard footsteps, but the only disturbances I'd seen in the dust were ones I'd made myself. I looked around one more time. I was suddenly cold, unsettled by what I'd discovered. I didn't want to sit through another creepy dinner tonight. More than anything, I wanted Jace beside me.

I retraced my steps as quickly as I could, descending the staircase all the way down to the butler's pantry and opening and closing the back door again so Eugenia would assume I came in from the outside. I found her in the kitchen.

"Eugenia?"

She poked her head out from the pantry.

"Oh, hello again, darling. I didn't hear you go back out—and without a coat? You must be freezing."

"I just needed a bit more air. And I was wondering... since tonight's dinner is so festive, and since Jace is practically a friend of the family these days, maybe we could invite him to join us?"

She covered her shock quickly with a signature wide smile.

"I'm not sure, dear—though that *would* make our place settings even." Eugenia placed her hand over her heart. "What am I saying? Of course, Jace is welcome. And I'm happy to let Sterling know of the plan, darling, but he might have his reservations."

I hadn't thought of Sterling's reaction. Speaking of things he'd specifically asked me not to do, I would imagine parading Jace around as my boyfriend would draw consequences if I wasn't careful. I wasn't ready for Sterling to kick me out, and I didn't want to get Jace fired, but I also wasn't going to pretend we weren't in a relationship. I was an adult, and Sterling couldn't realistically dictate my romantic attachments. We'd just have to skirt the line a bit.

"We're just spending a lot of time together, and it would be nice to have a friend around," I said cryptically.

"Well, of course, darling. When you say it like that, his presence makes perfect sense."

"I'll call him," I told her. "I don't have his number, though. I don't even know if he has a cell phone."

"I'm sure the Blackwells are in the book, dear."

"The book?"

"The phone book. We received the latest edition in January."

I'd never seen a phone book, but once Eugenia located it, I found two listings for J. Blackwell in the Astoria White Pages, same number. I used the house phone in the parlor. He answered on the third ring.

"Yeah?" he said into the line.

"Jace."

"Greer?" His tone softened, to my relief.

"Yes, it's Greer. Greer Richmond."

"I know who you are, sweetheart," he chuckled. "Is everything okay? I just got home."

"Everything is fine. I'm just calling because...I know you said we were going on a drive tomorrow, but there's going to be a dinner at the house tonight, and I wanted to invite you. It's at seven. You don't have to come if you don't want to, but Eugenia and Oren are coming over, and I thought it might be nice for you to come. If you want to," I reiterated.

Jace was silent for a few seconds.

"Does Eugenia know about this?"

"Yes," I said. "She thought it was a great idea."

"Sterling?"

"Yep," I lied. "Him too. But we need to be on our best behavior. I don't want you to get fired."

"It's going to be hard not to punch him in the face just for being a low-key creep in general, but with you, anything is possible."

I giggled, relieved. Gone was the tense, angry Jace and

his punishing kiss from the beach. In his place was Jace, my friend from the tarp. I'd have to get used to the mood swings.

"Is this a dress-up thing? Never mind. Do you want me to be there?"

"Yes," I whispered into the phone. "I want you to be there. I don't want to do this alone."

"Then I'm there."

He hung up.

~

I TOOK MY TIME IN THE BATHTUB, WASHING AND THEN BLOWING out my long hair before sitting in front of my mother's old-fashioned wooden vanity to do my makeup. I didn't wear makeup regularly, but I knew how to do a smoky eye, and I wanted to look my best tonight.

For Jace.

I was tired from my morning jaunt, and ever since I'd climbed down from the attic, I'd felt jumpy, like I was privy to information I shouldn't be privy to, and once Sterling found out, he'd confront me and my time at Richmond House would be over. I comforted myself with thoughts of Jace, how he'd kissed me, touched me, in a way that was both greedy and possessive but also somehow reverent. We'd crossed the line into a physical relationship, and I didn't know what it meant for us. Were we together? Dating? I knew enough about men to realize they didn't appreciate everything having to be labeled, but I was going to need some clarity.

I took a break from the whirling carousel of thoughts that had taken up residence in my brain and opened my wardrobe. I kept foldable clothes in the dresser and my slacks and other basics hanging in the closet, but this wardrobe held my most prized possessions—gifts from my mother. All the handbags, designer shoes, and beautiful dresses I could stuff into the four large suitcases I'd brought. Had I known what life in Astoria was like, I would have brought fewer dresses and more jeans and sweaters, but I wasn't sorry I had them to look at, to pull out and try on when I was feeling particularly lonely.

Dressing for dinner would be tricky. It was an occasion —though I couldn't tell you why we were suddenly having a dinner party—but I didn't want to look like I was trying too hard. I decided to go with black. A little black dress. There were several to choose from, but I pulled out a velvet Dolce and Gabbana with an off-the-shoulder sweetheart neckline. Black was classic. Sophisticated. I skipped the heels since they would surely dig into the hardwood floors, and I didn't want to spend the evening playing Hot Lava Monster, trying to make sure I was always on a rug. Instead, I wore my favorite patent black wedges and took one last look in the mirror.

My makeup was heavy—I'd broken the cardinal rule of pairing a smoky eye with a pale lip. Instead, I'd done a red lip, and it contrasted nicely with my pale hair and skin and black dress. I looked older. There was still an hour to go before dinner, but I knew Sterling was likely already serving drinks to Eugenia and Oren. I hoped Jace knew to come a bit early.

The doors to the parlor were open when I got to the bottom of the stairs. Tinny music from an old gramophone in the corner provided a lovely backdrop to the scene I walked in on. Sterling and Oren were dressed formally and lounging side by side in matching wingback chairs, scotches in hand. Eugenia had arranged herself on one of the chaises in a way that was fetching, but casual. She held a martini glass in her hand, the three large olives magnified inside the clear liquid. The woman Eugenia slapped at the forest's edge sat on the chaise across from her. She wore a white silk sheath with an oriental collar that drew attention to her waif-like frame.

When I moved farther into the room, my grandfather and Oren stood to greet me.

"Good evening, Greer," Eugenia called out. "You look absolutely beautiful tonight. Like a petal on a rose, the bloom of youth..." she trailed off, taking a greedy sip of her drink.

"Thank you, Eugenia. Hi," I said, turning toward the other woman and extending my hand. "I'm Greer."

"Anna," she said flatly, not bothering to shake. Sterling swung his head and blasted her with a furious look. She finally held up her hand, limp and cold, and draped it over mine before snatching it away again.

"Darling, don't be rude," Eugenia recovered. "You're a guest in this house, remember? Greer, Anna is my daughter. I believe she must be just a few years older than you."

"Well, it's nice to meet you in person. I've heard a lot about you."

"From Jace?" she asked, her face taking on a comically hopeful expression.

"From Jace, sure...and from Oren," I said diplomatically. Well, that was an interesting development. Could she *be* any more obvious about her crush?

"Greer?" Sterling interrupted, placing his hand on my lower back to escort me to the bar. "Would you like wine, or...?"

"Just club soda with lime is fine." I couldn't stand to look at him, couldn't stand to have his hands on me. Suddenly, the room felt overly warm, with the knowledge of Eugenia and Sterling's alleged affair, Anna's parentage,

Sterling's proclivities, and Oren's enabling all competing in my mind for traction.

He fixed my drink, and I used the opportunity to bring up Jace.

"Thank you for allowing Jace to come tonight." I hoped Eugenia had told him.

"We—that is, both Eugenia and I—are glad you've made a friend here." He lowered his voice. "As long as that's all he is, Greer."

"Of course," I answered automatically, ashamed that I hadn't just announced that Jace and I were together. What was I afraid of?

A heavy chime sounded, so loud it startled me, and I almost dropped the glass Sterling had handed me seconds before.

"That would be Mr. Blackwell," Eugenia said, standing elegantly, belying the way she was downing her cocktail. "I'll show him in."

She sauntered out of the room and down the hall to the wide double doors at the front entrance. I saw Anna sit up a little straighter on the chaise and smooth her dress before I trailed behind Eugenia. Jace was in for a surprise.

Eugenia opened one of the big front doors wide from the inside, the awful shudder immediately replaced in my mind by the sight of Jace standing on the porch. Lit from behind by the sunset and dressed in black suit pants and a white button-down, his black hair combed back, I couldn't look away.

When he saw me, he nodded at Eugenia's greeting before stepping around her and walking down the hallway toward me. He'd told me he'd only been inside Richmond House once, on the day Sterling called him into his office, but he didn't bother looking around. He didn't care about the architecture or the windows, the crown molding, or the original antique furnishings. He only had eyes for me.

I could feel his gaze like a kiss as it landed heavily on my hair, the planes of my face, and my red lips before dropping to my bare collarbone and dipping into my cleavage. We stood that way, devouring each other without touching or saying a word until Sterling cleared his throat from the parlor doorway.

"Welcome, Mr. Blackwell. Glad you could join us."

"Thank you for inviting me."

Eugenia followed us back into the parlor after securing the front doors. Oren, clearly enjoying his drink, hadn't bothered to move from his spot in the chair.

"Jace!" he called out in his typical friendly greeting. "How are you, boy? How's the old man? Need us to rustle you up a jacket? Dinner is formal; didn't Greer tell you?"

"Oren!"

"I'm sorry," Jace spoke directly to Oren. "This is my suit from Junior Prom, and the jacket doesn't fit me anymore. It was either this or my dress whites."

"That's right—forgot about your time in the service."

"You were in the military?" I asked.

"I was in the navy. It's not important. We can talk about it later."

"Well, I think you look amazing," I whispered.

"You look gorgeous, Jace, as always," Anna echoed from her inconspicuous perch on the chaise. Gone was the rude, childish girl from five minutes ago. In her place was a confident woman who knew what she wanted. Or whom.

My man.

Jace stiffened beside me at Anna's words.

"Still, it's a formal dinner," Oren continued, a bit too loudly. "Sterling, maybe you have a jacket upstairs he could borrow."

"I'm afraid I don't share Mr. Blackwell's immense measurements, Oren," Sterling said. His voice and manner were civil if a bit cool, but thankfully he didn't seem set on humiliating Jace. "We will simply remove our jackets for dinner if it bothers you that much."

Oren snorted at that.

"Would you like a drink?" Sterling asked Jace.

"No, thank you, sir."

"Water? A club soda?"

"I'm fine."

"Tell me, Blackwell," Sterling said, leading both of us back to the center of the room, "how are things going in our makeshift shipyard?" Jace quickly seated himself beside Eugenia, leaving me to take the spot beside Anna, who tucked her skirt under her like any part of her that came into contact with me meant certain death.

"You've got a real beauty on your hands in that old Chris-Craft in the garage. She's been my main focus this past year, and she should be seaworthy by the summer." Jace's face became more animated, and his deep voice sounded almost boyish as he talked about the yacht.

"You've done an admirable job with her," Sterling said, sipping his scotch. "I can only hope you continue to make yourself available to work on the project."

Jace nodded.

"And what about our secondary endeavor—the one Eugenia took it upon herself to commission? How is that shaping up? I'm hoping for another report from you soon."

Jace lowered his eyes to his shoes and ran his palms down the legs of his slacks.

"What endeavor?" I asked.

"It's nothing, dear. Mr. Blackwell just owes me a conversation about...a maintenance project."

"Oren," I said, changing the subject and drawing Oren's

attention away from the bottom of his glass. "Jace and I visited the wreck of the *Jonathan Richmond* this morning."

"Our darling Greer is working on a school project about it," Eugenia added. "Isn't that just super?"

Jace locked eyes with me and smiled in encouragement. Everyone else just melted away as I stared into his black depths for a few seconds. I turned my head back toward Oren just in time to witness Sterling's cold, pointed look. He knew.

"I was wondering if we could make an appointment with you to talk about it," I continued.

"Well, what about it?" Oren tipped his glass back and forth, the ice rattling against the crystal. "There's no time like the present. Never know when a day will be your last."

Eugenia lifted a silent toast.

"Well...okay...so we couldn't find much on the wreck in the library, which was strange because almost every other Oregon Coast shipwreck was well-documented there in the archives."

Oren and Sterling exchanged a look I couldn't decipher.

"But I was using my laptop, and I came across a historian with a book on the wreck. The library ordered it for me, and it turns out this historian...he seemed to think..."

Oren opened his mouth to speak, but Sterling interjected.

"I think I have a good idea of what you're going to ask, and it's not true. I don't mind telling you that I find this conversation incredibly distasteful, Greer, and I won't tolerate any slandering of the Richmond name under this roof."

Now it was our eyes that locked, but in a standoff. He didn't want to talk about our family's alleged role in the slave trade? Then I'm guessing he *really* didn't want to talk about my suspicion that he sexually abused his own daughter. Daughters. At best, his mental and emotional abuse had no doubt turned them into needy, walking skeletons. I looked at Anna, who seemed delighted that Sterling had scolded me. It was on the tip of my tongue to tell him off once and for all and get the hell out of this toxic environment when he stood up.

"Eugenia, it's early, but I find myself rather hungry, and I'd like to eat now."

With that, all six members of our uncomfortable dinner party made our way down the vast hall from the parlor to the dining room. Eugenia had changed the table runner in anticipation of the coming season, and bits of dried lavender stuck to the floral brocade.

Eugenia and I flanked Sterling, who was once again seated at the head of the table. Anna sat next to Eugenia and across from Oren, who sat beside me. Jace took the remaining seat on the other side of Oren. His position prevented us from speaking, and the air was thick with stilted conversation throughout the meal. Anna was the only one who bothered to make small talk, taking full advantage of her position near Jace. She ate nothing, instead peppering him with benign questions and anecdotes about their time together at Astoria High School that made it sound like they'd been the best of friends. Jace answered politely but never initiated conversation with her, clearly uncomfortable with Anna's hero worship. I couldn't wait for dinner to be over.

Eugenia served the dessert course, reseated herself, and began tapping the side of her glass with her knife.

Sterling rolled his eyes.

"Attention, everyone. Sterling and I have an announcement."

I sat back in my chair, unsure where this was going.

"I confess, this dinner wasn't spontaneous, but a venue

to share our very important news with our family and closest friend. And you too, Jace."

I glanced at him in time to see him lift his eyebrow. I stifled another giggle.

"Anyway, what I'm trying to say is that Sterling and I... are to wed! At the end of the summer!"

It took a few seconds for what Eugenia had said to register. Sterling was marrying Eugenia? Their rumored affair flashed in my mind, but I'd never personally seen them show any sort of affection for one another. I hadn't even ever seen them together except for tonight and the night I arrived at Richmond House. I smiled automatically, but it felt fake. Whatever this was, they weren't getting married because they were in love.

"Wonderful news, Gerry!" Oren said awkwardly. It made me feel better that he had no idea what to make of this either. Jace filled the resulting silence with a slow clap that Oren and I soon joined, the three of us applauding like madmen as Eugenia and Anna beamed. Sterling seemed on the verge of trading his usual stoic expression for one of complete boredom.

"Yes, well, it was time," he said to stop the clapping.

"I'm sure we'll be very happy together, darling. We're going to be a real family now," Eugenia said to him.

Watching Eugenia watch Sterling with pride—and watching him stare straight ahead—made me even more uneasy. Nothing made sense in this house. I was ready for the night to be over.

"I'm tired," I announced to no one in particular.

Jace pushed up and out of his chair at my words.

Oren, too, stood up. "If it's all the same to you lovebirds, I'll let Greer walk me out as well. Thank you for an exhilarating evening, Sterling. I'm happy for you, friends."

Oren threw his napkin on his plate, and Jace and I

followed him to the pantry where the wide exterior door sat ready to aid in our escape. Stepping out into the night, closing the door firmly behind us, I felt myself relax for the first time that evening.

It was a cool, breezy spring night. Jace and I stood on the porch, wanting a moment of privacy, but Oren turned back to us, not taking the hint.

"About what Sterling said in there..." he began.

"Which part?" I blew out on a choked laugh. "The part where he had the nerve to snap at me for asking about our family's dubious history or the part where he announced his engagement to a woman he's indifferent to?"

"Uh, the former, I guess. But don't worry about Gerry. She'll see that you're well taken care of."

"What do you mean?"

"Just that if she marries Sterling, she'll inherit Richmond House. Not you."

I leaned into Jace as realization struck. I hadn't even considered the idea that I would inherit money or a house from Sterling, though it made sense. Right now, I was his next of kin. Unless he'd already written me out of the will, but Sterling was a traditionalist if nothing else. He'd want a Richmond to inherit his fortune. Maybe that's why he was marrying Eugenia—if Anna was his biological daughter, she would own Richmond House someday.

"I don't care about that, Oren," I said, refusing to dwell on how much money I currently stood to gain. "I don't even want this house. What were you going to tell us before?"

"Only that there may be some truth to the slave-trade allegations, though you'd better not bring it up with Sterling again. And don't pay any mind to anything you read about the house itself."

"The house itself? This house?"

"There's a couple of folks in town...political rivals who

aren't fans of your granddad's business tactics, who've been spreading rumors for years—decades, really—about how the men in your family might have used the house as... quarters...for captured slaves coming off the boats before they could arrange for their passage to their new masters."

I'm sure my face was a mask of shock because Oren plowed on hurriedly.

"As I said, I doubt that's true. The running of slaves, maybe. But I doubt any Richmond would have kept slaves in his own house."

Oren turned once again and disappeared into the darkness toward his parked Mercedes. I refused to think about what I'd seen in the attic. I couldn't right now. I wondered if Eugenia was spending the night. I didn't know why, but the thought disgusted me. The idea that she and Anna might leave and drive back to their own place disgusted me more. I'd never had a problem with Eugenia. She was brittle and fake at times, but I remembered the moments of kindness she'd shown when I'd arrived, and I'd grown fond of her. Still, what kind of woman married a man who was clearly not interested in her? For a house? For money? That I didn't understand.

Jace wrapped his arms around me, resting his chin against my forehead. When I'd offered to walk him out, I'd envisioned passionate kissing, but now I was reeling, and he seemed to sense it.

"I'll be back in the morning," he murmured before releasing me. "Are you okay here?"

"Yeah, I'm fine. But it's getting harder and harder to be around him knowing..."

"I know. Just give me another few weeks—months at most—to get my place. Once you're out of here, we can decide what to do."

"I'm already way past the 'couple of weeks' mark Sterling mentioned when he invited me. I don't have months..." I trailed off. "And what about Anna? She seems pretty...into you."

"I'm sorry. I didn't know she was going to be here, or I would have told you—she ambushed me in the library the other day when I went alone. She told me she'd liked me since high school, and she wanted to date me."

I didn't appreciate Anna's attitude toward me, but it made sense now.

"And you told her you weren't interested, or...?"

"I told her I was seeing someone. I told her I had a girlfriend."

"A girlfriend, huh?" I smiled. "You want me to be your girlfriend? You'll have to ask me nicely."

Jace's expression turned serious. For a second, I thought he was kidding around, that he was going to get on one knee and ask me in a completely over-the-top gesture meant to mimic a marriage proposal, but he just studied my face before taking my hand in his.

"Greer Richmond, I've never had a girlfriend. I don't know how to be in a relationship. But I've never...felt...like this. Like I belong to someone, and she belongs to me. I've never felt much of anything before, except disappointment and anger. I want to be with you. Officially."

It wasn't a pretty speech, but I felt my eyes burn as I processed what he'd said. He wanted to be with me. I made him feel things.

He shoved his hands in his pockets and thumped down the simple wooden steps in heavy strides before he, too, disappeared into the dark. I wrapped my bare arms around myself in a practiced gesture and looked up at the sky. When I heard rustling grass in the distance, I lowered my head to peer out into the grassy field beyond the house, looking for the source. Trails of thick fog curled around the knife-edged bottoms of the ships propped up in the field, the tendrils making them look like they were floating down the River Styx on their way to hell. I couldn't see anything, but I swore I heard something moving stealthily through the grass.

I walked a few steps closer. I didn't want to get too close in case it was a snake. Or a spider. A giant spider that could make grass rustle.

I smiled to myself.

I might be a city girl, but even I knew we didn't have grass-rustling snakes and spiders in the Pacific Northwest. It was probably a deer walking peacefully through the field, enjoying a near-midnight snack.

Suddenly, the nearest wall of grass split in two, and Garbage the Goose charged with everything he was worth. I let out an involuntary shriek, frozen to the spot in shock for several precious seconds before I turned and ran back to the steps and through the back door.

What the hell was wrong with that animal? Seriously?

I leaned against the back door and waited for my heart rate to slow before making my way back through the dining room. It was empty, no sign of Sterling or Eugenia, the remnants of our dinner party still on the table. The hall and staircase were dark, with no light coming from any of the downstairs rooms. Upstairs, Sterling's door was closed, and I couldn't hear any conversation as I walked past.

Exhausted, I turned the key in my door and locked myself in. I shimmied out of my dress and used a washcloth from the caddy I'd retrieved from the hallway earlier and the water pitcher in the corner of the room to remove my makeup. Sliding under the covers, I turned onto my back and listened to the familiar, distant sounds of the large, old house settling in for another night—until the squeal of footsteps directly above my head caused my heart once again to try pounding its way out of my chest.

I kept still. There was no way I was investigating again at this time of night. In fact, I decided here and now I wasn't going to venture into the attic ever again, trunk-love be damned. I might never leave this room. The sound of the footsteps faded before they came back full force. Who was up there? It sounded like one person. Sterling? Eugenia? What if they fell through the ceiling on top of me?

I made myself smaller in bed, pulled the covers tighter, trying to remember whether it was the little-girl bed or the barrack-looking things that were directly above me, but I couldn't remember the attic layout in relation to my room. The sounds eventually stopped. I fell into a restless sleep, my stomach sick with dread at the thought of tomorrow.

17
JACE

It'd been a week since I'd kissed Greer on the beach and gone to dinner at Richmond House, a week spent with my tongue inside her mouth and my hands somewhere on her skin. Sterling had left on a business trip days ago—probably a good thing, considering how I couldn't focus on work. I wasn't going to pump Greer for information to report back, either. Not anymore. Besides, today wasn't about taking from her. Today, I wanted to give.

Today was April fourteenth, the day Greer turned twenty-one. All she wanted, she said, was to spend the day with me. With Sterling gone, there was no need to sneak into her bedroom. She let me in, and I sprinted up the stairs, dragging her behind me as she laughed. Eugenia rarely showed up to fix meals when Sterling wasn't in residence, even though Greer still needed to eat. It bothered me, but I kept my mouth shut and brought her dinner when I could.

In her room, I turned the old-fashioned key in the lock and looked around. The furniture was all heavy, dark wood. It contrasted with the bright floral of her bedspread. Behind her, through the windows, I could see the deep blue of the river.

I hadn't had sex since well before Greer showed up on the scene, and all our messing around had left me hard up. For the first time in my life, I wanted a woman so badly that no amount of jacking off in my room in the trailer could assuage my lust. I needed more of her. I didn't want to see slivers of her skin; I wanted to see all of it. I wanted to taste her. Today was the day, but I needed to take things slow.

We hadn't discussed it yet, but I liked my sex rough. I wanted women face down, ass up while I pounded into them, sucking and biting, taking out my anger on them. They seemed to enjoy it—but I knew I couldn't do that with Greer. At least not yet. She'd told me she wasn't a virgin, but with the quick, clumsy coupling she'd described as her only experience, she might as well have been. I'd vowed then and there to make today all about her.

"Happy Birthday, sweetheart," I said to her, slowly stalking her along the perimeter of the room. I'd forgotten the necklace I'd gotten her in the car. It was a single pearl on a gold chain. I'd found it in one of the antique shops in town. I should run down and get it, but wild horses couldn't drag me away from this moment. "Got you a present, but I'll give it to you later."

"I thought you were my present."

Greer gave me a wide smile, suddenly shy, her finger absently tapping patterns on her thigh. She was nervous. As much as I'd like to initiate right away, I told myself again that I had to slow down. It had to be her decision to go further than we'd gone before. I decided to sit on the bed and let her make the first move.

She didn't waste any time coming up to me. She took the bottom of my black T-shirt into her hands and tugged it like she wanted it off. I obliged, grasping the fabric behind my head and pulling it off my torso. Despite telling myself not to play an active role in this seduction just seconds before, I couldn't help myself. I lifted her thin tank top over her head to reveal a white mesh bra that left nothing to the imagination before unbuttoning her jeans and getting an eyeful of her matching panties—and what was underneath.

I pulled her so she was straddling me, her cleft perfectly aligned with my hard cock through my jeans and boxers. She instinctively began to grind her wet panties against me, searching for friction.

But it wasn't enough. She needed more.

I stood, picking her up and reversing our positions. I backed her up to the bed before gently laying her back and kneeling on the rug in front of her. She leaned back on her elbows, and I peeled her panties down her smooth, pale legs before I spread them wide, revealing her succulent flesh.

As slowly as I could, I placed wet kisses and love bites on the insides of her thighs, sucking gently on the delicate crease where her legs met her pelvis. God, she smelled good.

Greer moaned, throwing her head back and moving her hips instinctually, trying to position my tongue nearer her clit, but I held her in place and continued to slowly kiss her everywhere but where she wanted me to, building the anticipation.

Smiling, I finally swiped my tongue directly over her swollen bud, and she gasped.

"I'll make you a deal, birthday girl. I want you to look at me while I lick your pussy."

"Wh...what?"

"I want you to look at me, and while you're looking at me, I'll do anything you want."

When she lifted her head and met my eyes, I realized I

was closer to coming than I should be, considering my pants were still on. Tousled ponytail. Swollen lips from the way she was biting them. And eyes like honey, so needy they looked on the verge of tears. Not to mention the fact that the thin bra she was wearing did little to conceal the perfect teardrop shape of her breasts or the size and shape of her pink nipples.

I leaned forward and took one in my mouth, wetting the delicate mesh covering it. I moved to the other side and did the same, alternating breasts once more before I opened the front clasp of the bra, and her smooth globes popped out of the restrictive fabric. Laying Greer flat on her back, I loomed over her, sucking hard, first on one perfect nipple, then the other until she was undulating her hips against mine.

With a final wet suction sound, I returned to my previous position in front of her splayed-open legs and waited. Lifting back onto her elbows, her eyes connected with mine. As soon as they did, I applied the same wet suction to her clit. As soon as she broke eye contact, I stopped.

"Ugh," she said, frustrated, wiggling her hips.

"You know the deal, sweetheart."

We locked eyes again, and I resumed licking and sucking her tender folds, circling her clit with my tongue until she couldn't hold back the unconscious words that began streaming out of her mouth.

I knew she was close when she got quiet again. I'd lost my virginity at fourteen, and giving oral was a skill I hadn't minded developing over the years. I kept my strokes consistent, making sure each one circled over her little nub. When her hips started moving involuntarily, I sucked her clit into my mouth and swirled over it in a series of tight little circles.

She came sharply, arching her back and digging her fingers into my hair, holding my mouth away from her now-sensitive flesh. Goddamn, she was beautiful.

She lowered back down onto the bed, the ragged saw of her chest causing her perfect tits to move slightly with her breathing. I kept my face between her legs, not touching her, but warming her with my breath and enjoying the scent of her climax. Finally, I placed a kiss on either side of her thighs before pushing my large body up off the uncomfortable wooden floor and stretching out on the bed beside her. For a minute, I thought she'd fallen asleep. Until she reached for the button of my jeans.

"Don't even think about it, sweetheart," I said, pushing her hand away.

"But I want to."

"And I want you to, but it's not happening today. Today is your day. It's all about you."

"Well, if it's all about me, I should get to do what I want."

I couldn't keep the smile off my face. She had me there. Lying in bed with her was too tempting—it would be so easy to lose my jeans and watch her pleasure me with her mouth, so easy to pull her over me so that her soaked pussy was on top of my bare cock, so easy to push inside and lose myself. I needed to get off this bed.

I adjusted my throbbing cock as I stood up.

"Wait—are you leaving?" she asked. I heard insecurity in her voice, but also acceptance. As if she accepted the fact that after what had just happened between us, I'd be done and want to leave her behind. Accepted the fact that no one cared enough about her to stay. I didn't like it.

"Sweetheart, I could find out the powers that be were dropping a nuclear bomb, and this room was ground zero, and I still wouldn't leave."

She smiled then, feeling reassured that I wasn't going to just cut and run. I wandered around the room, picking up each bottle of perfume from her dresser and making exaggerated sniffing noises, which made her laugh. I'd been in feminine bedrooms before—from the neighborhood girls' dank rooms in the backs of their doublewides to the plush master bedrooms of women twice my age. I'd never cared about anything before but the sex, but I was fascinated with Greer's space. Her dresser, topped with a gold-rimmed oval tray where she set her perfumes, hairbrush, and jewelry box. An old-fashioned vanity framed in dark wood where she'd neatly laid out her makeup. I wandered across the room and opened the wardrobe, inhaling Greer's light floral scent on the dresses inside—dresses in every color of the rainbow, some plain, some covered in sequins. There weren't places to wear these types of clothes in Astoria. There weren't going to be places to wear them for a very long time if she stayed with me.

With that depressing thought in mind, I reached my final destination—a rolltop desk tucked into the corner below one of the windows. Here was the only place in the room that was the least bit messy—a large envelope lay ripped open and discarded, the paperwork inside fanned out alongside. I glanced at the block address at the top of the first page, curious but not wanting to intrude. The University of Washington in Seattle. A course catalog for Greer's fall quarter. She needed to register soon. The knot in my stomach that had formed while I was looking at the dresses intensified.

"Don't worry about that," Greer said. She'd located her panties on the floor and pulled them up her legs. I watched over my shoulder as her pussy disappeared beneath the fabric, my semihard cock once again thickening to full mast.

She came up behind me and wrapped her arms around my torso. She could barely get her hands around to my pecs, much less wrap me in a hug.

"You can come with me," she said.

"Come with you?"

"Yeah, I've been thinking about it. We could live in my mom's apartment in the city. You could get a job. A good-paying job, like at the shipyard. And you could go to school."

Her offer was tempting. I wanted to accept, wanted to promise to find a way to make it work, but I knew I couldn't. Even with all my savings and a job, I didn't think I could afford to live in an expensive city like Seattle long-term and attend a university. There was no way I could afford it *and* give Greer the lifestyle she was used to. Plus, I had Jesse to consider. Paying for someone to look in on him once a day was one thing, but having to manage everything from up north—there was no way. Greer sensed my hesitation.

"Fine, it's settled. I'll just stay here. That would be better anyway, I think."

"Sweetheart, of course you need to finish school."

"I can finish school anywhere. I just want us to be together. Things are different now than they were before, right?"

"Right," I said. But they weren't different, not really. Whatever feelings I had for Greer weren't going to keep her here. I didn't want them to. Greer didn't belong in a trailer park in Astoria, Oregon, or even a regular apartment. She'd make the right decision in the end, and I'd live with it. I just needed to enjoy the time we did have together and encourage her to dump me and spread her wings when the time came.

She tried to turn my body so that we were facing each

other, but she couldn't move me unless I cooperated. Erasing what I was sure was disapproval from my face at the thought of Greer wasting away in Astoria on my behalf, I finally turned to face her.

She smiled at me, a ponytail holding her heavy hair away from her face so I could take in her perfectly proportioned features. She was so fucking beautiful, and the more time we spent together, the less I understood how anyone could care about anything more than they cared about her —her father, her mother, now Sterling...everyone she'd ever known had just left her on her own. I could barely leave her alone to eat and sleep.

I'd never abandon her. The thought popped into my head, and even though we'd only known each other for a little more than a month, nothing had ever felt as right to me. Even if we broke up—when we broke up—I couldn't imagine ever not choosing her.

She went up on her toes to kiss me; she didn't pull back when she tasted herself on my lips like I expected. She deepened the kiss, and I groaned into her mouth.

"I've created a monster," I said against her lips.

Again, she reached for my jeans.

"I want to...taste you now."

Jesus fucking Christ.

She wasn't ready for that. Hell, I wasn't ready.

"Not today, birthday girl. I have a better idea." I playfully swatted her hand away, rejecting her, but trying to take away the sting. "What about a field trip? I've decided I need another tattoo."

18
GREER

A bell rang over the door of the tattoo parlor as Jace pushed it open. There were dozens of tattoo shops in Astoria. I had no idea why Jace chose this one for his other tattoos, but he wanted a repeat, so the work must be good.

The black-and-white checkered floor gave the place a retro feel, and each station in the open-concept shop had its own unique look, almost like the chairs and tables were salvaged and repurposed. If we were in Portland or back in Seattle, I'd say the owners had carefully manufactured the whole "edgy but cohesive" look for the hipster crowd, but in an out-of-the-way alley on the north side of Astoria, it was authentic. This place catered to the real deal—sailors, laborers, and blue-collar workers of all kinds.

I paused to look at the artists' work showcased on the shop's walls at the entrance. Above the basic designs of hearts, flowers, and various cute sea creatures were framed galleries depicting geometric nature scenes, simple, vintage-looking nautical and military symbols, and swirling Asian-inspired imagery where sumo wrestlers squared off or lotus flowers floated in lily ponds. Each artist seemed to have their unique style, and I wondered what Jace would choose.

Jace turned back toward me from the counter where he'd been taking care of his deposit.

"You can sit with me while I'm getting worked on, but I want the final result to be a surprise, so stay here for a minute."

"Okay." I plopped into a bright orange chair to wait.

I watched Jace head to the back of the shop where he shook hands with a man who looked much older—closer to Sterling's age. They turned toward a table situated against a wall, and Jace started talking while the man located his drawing pencil. The man smiled at whatever Jace was saying and turned his head to look at me across the shop, nodding and putting pencil to paper. It only took a few minutes of drawing—with Jace pointing things out occasionally—to complete the stencil. I couldn't make out what it was, but it looked small. The man placed the stencil onto the right side of Jace's chest, pulling it off before situating Jace onto a chair facing the wall and beckoning me over.

"Good morning, little lady," he said. "Jace tells me your name is Greer. I'm Jack."

"Hi, yes. Nice to meet you."

"Just stay behind me, sweetheart," Jace said. "I want this to be a surprise."

I smiled, but inside my head, I was racking my brain. Maybe it was a boat, like the one he was on when we'd met. Maybe it was a paint can.

I giggled.

"She laughs at my pain," Jace said, wincing, as the whirring of the needle started up.

"No, just wondering what the surprise is."

"You'll know soon enough," he said over his shoulder.

I was left to stare at the broad, smooth expanse of his

bare back, once again experiencing a type of lust that was new to me. I wasn't a prude by any means. I'd had crushes on boys back at school and even participated in the occasional spin-the-bottle kiss at parties. I'd gone on a few lackluster dates during my college years, had sex, and I even had a vibrator that I'd used regularly in Seattle, but I was too scared to fire it up within the tomb-like walls of Richmond House where even the smallest sound could produce an echo that resonated. The last thing I needed was Eugenia—or Sterling—coming to investigate. The thought sickened me.

No, the way I felt when I was with Jace didn't compare. It was sheer adrenaline, like touching a live wire. It burned through me, making the tips of my fingers and toes buzz with excitement. Every time we were together, constantly now, I wanted some part of my skin touching some part of his. I wanted to please him, but so far, he hadn't seemed interested in anything more than our kissing and heavy petting. At least until this morning when he made me come on his tongue.

I blushed, thinking of the way I'd spread my legs and watched him place his mouth on me. It was so...intimate. So dirty, and yet, so tender. Like he was honored when really it should have been me thanking him. I watched the muscles of his back tighten as he chased away the pain. I wished I could peel off my tank top, unhook my bra, and press my bare breasts into his back the way I did earlier. I wanted to lick the single bead of sweat that was forming on the back of his neck. I couldn't believe what had happened to me—to us—in just six short weeks.

"You're quiet back there," he said to me over the whir of the machine.

"Just thinking about things."

He turned his head around to look at me, and I blushed.

"What sort of things?"

"Just...things."

"I think I'm going to like hearing about those things later."

It took almost two hours, but the time passed quickly. There was so much to look at.

"All finished," Jack said. He wiped down Jace's chest with a cloth.

"Come take a look, little lady, before I bandage him up."

Jace shifted in his chair, avoiding eye contact as I came around him to look at the tattoo.

Jack had tattooed the right side of his chest, and the finished image was about the size of a fist. It depicted a minimalist flower done in one continuous line that reminded me of the flower Jace had woven for me out of that single blade of grass in the field after my near-death experience. At the center of the petal-laden bloom, the swirling loops of the line came together to form a beautiful cursive "G."

I stared at the tattoo, in awe of Jack's incredible skill, slowly realizing the letter's significance. Why would he want to surprise me unless that "G" stood for "Greer?" For me.

I raised my eyes to meet his, and he shot me a cocky grin.

"Don't get a big head. I just wanted to keep you close. Make sure I would always remember you."

Horrified at the sudden urge to burst into tears, all I could do was smile. I couldn't think of anything witty to say back. He was trying to keep it light, and I appreciated it, but I couldn't control my emotions. No one had ever wanted to keep me with them.

Jace seemed to sense my thoughts because he took it

upon himself to make small talk with Jack as he was wrapping him up.

"You know the drill, J," Jack said. "Give it a quick rinse this afternoon. No swimming. Wear a shirt in the sun until it heals."

"Thanks, Jack. You're an artist."

Jace put his shirt back on, and the two men shook hands and slapped each other on the back before Jace moved to the front counter to pay.

"It was nice to meet you, Greer. I've never known Jace to be a sentimental boy. You must be someone exceptional."

I smiled at him, still not ready to form words. Jace and I walked out together and stood in the alley in front of the shop.

"What do you want to do now?" he asked. I was thankful that he didn't seem to want to talk about the significance of the tattoo. We both knew what it meant, but saying it out loud might cheapen it somehow.

"I want to see where you live," I finally said.

"Not a good idea, sweetheart."

"I just want to—"

"No."

I stilled at this harsh reaction, and he softened.

"You don't know what you're asking. Please don't make me."

"Then how about ice cream?" I teased.

"That we can do. Since it's your birthday and all."

19
JACE

There was no way in hell I was taking Greer to the trailer. No way. I wouldn't take her there even if Jesse was still in the hospital and we had the place to ourselves. Even though I knew it probably wouldn't happen, I couldn't shake the feeling that she'd take one look at the place and never speak to me again. Or maybe she would, but she'd never see me the same way. Our relationship would change for the worse if she ever saw who I really was. Right now, I was trash. Even if I could better myself, I was never going to be the kind of guy someone like Greer ended up with. There was always a chance, but I vowed again to enjoy being with her while I could.

I pulled up to the trailer after I'd dropped Greer back at Richmond House and tried to see it the way Greer would if she were sitting beside me now. It had rusted. Faded. The inside was as clean as I could keep it, but I didn't have time to repair all the rust spots and corroded metal clinging to the joints and undercarriage. The lawn—if you could call it that—was equally depressing. Mainly because right in the middle of it, sitting in a lawn chair that was hanging on by a thread, was Jesse. Passed out. Beer bottles sprinkled around him as if he were an installation art piece titled "Drunk Man."

He'd been out of the hospital for less than a day, and he was already at it. I had no idea where he'd gotten the booze, but drunks are resourceful like that.

"Blackwell!"

I looked across the road toward the shout and saw Linus standing in his yard, beckoning me. I went over.

"What's up?"

"That favor you asked me for? Done and done, man."

"Oh yeah?"

"Yeah, you were right. I just told my guy that I had a friend who needed some information, and he pulled it for me right away. He didn't care."

"Do you have it with you?"

"No, man, he just pulled it up on the computer right quick and let me look. I didn't want to be high maintenance, you know?"

"Okay, so what did it say?"

"Nothing much. I don't know what you were looking for, but the only thing on one Sterling Richmond's criminal record was a complaint from some girl's parents."

Jackpot.

"Which girl? What was the complaint?"

"They sealed the details up tight, man, sorry. She was a minor, I guess. My cop friend couldn't get anything else on it."

"Fuck."

"Yeah. Sorry."

"Was there anything else? Any other detail you can remember."

"Not really...except that whatever charge he caught, it was old. If you're after more info on some new crime, this wasn't it."

"How do you know it wasn't recent?"

"Settlement date. Cops charged this Sterling dude, but he settled out of court. In 1969."

Linus said I didn't owe him anything then and there for the information, just a favor if he ever needed one. I crossed back and skipped the two splintered steps that acted as a boost to the door of my trailer. At my size, I just took a big step up and heaved myself inside.

Taking my weekly cash from Sterling—minus the funds for the tattoo—out of my wallet, I located the hollowed-out encyclopedia in my bookshelf where I hid my money. I was so close to a different life. A life I could be proud of. A life Greer might want to come back to after she finished college—if I did enough. Just a few more weeks.

I pulled the book from my bookshelf and opened it, but in the hollow where a gallon-sized plastic bag had held almost $30,000 in hundred-dollar bills, there was nothing.

"What the fuck?" The sick thud of my heartbeat flared in my chest. I looked around the room, as if I could've misplaced the money somewhere else. Had I been robbed? Nothing looked out of place. Then I remembered Jesse. And the beer.

I felt it in the back of my spine first, the chill. A feeling so cold, but so hot. So painful. Like the precious seconds after you stick your hand through a flame before your body registers the pain. I was going to kill him.

I ripped the trailer's door back open and jumped down into the weed-filled lawn, headed straight for Jesse, still passed out in his chair. Thankfully, the crack of my fist against his face was enough to rouse him.

"Where is it? Where's my fucking money?"

The blow knocked him over in the chair, and he was slow to get up, drunk and uncoordinated.

He finally stood and faced me, wearing a shit-eating grin.

"And a good afternoon to you too, boy. Where you been at?"

"It's none of your fucking business where I go. Where's my money?"

"What money?" He smirked, and it took everything I had not to hit him again. But I didn't want to risk knocking him out cold and not being able to recover what I could of my nest egg.

"The money you stole from me. Give it up now, or I'll make you wish that you had."

"Such disrespect." Jesse shook his head, putting on the show for the neighbors that had come out onto their sad front stoops to watch the drama. "Just look at the way he treats his old man."

"I'll be treating you a lot worse if you don't start talking. Now, where is it?"

He paused for dramatic effect. As if this were a white-trash production of Macbeth.

"It's gone."

"No. You couldn't have spent $30,000 on beer in the past twelve hours. You're hiding it somewhere."

"Son, I did it for us. I was going through your room for a bit of beer money—you wouldn't begrudge your old man a ten-spot to buy himself a beer after weeks in that goddamn hospital, would you? When I found it, I knew what I had to do. I had to protect you. Selling drugs, sucking dick—however you're making that money, it has to stop."

"What. Did. You. Do with the money, Jesse?"

"I invested it for you. Gave it to Dave down at the Blue Spur. He's going to use it to fix that spot in the bar where he tried to knock the wall down. Said he'll give us ten percent ownership in the place in exchange."

I stared him down, fighting back tears. My hands clenched into fists. I couldn't believe it. Everything I'd saved for years, gone in an instant. Because of Jesse. Everything bad was because of Jesse.

"Did you sign a contract with Dave?" I choked out. "Do you even know Dave's last name?"

"Don't need to know it." Jesse ambled over to his overturned lawn chair and righted it before collapsing into the seat. "Dave is a man of his word. Unlike you."

The words had barely left his lips before I was on him. This time, I launched my whole body at him and tackled him out of the chair. Straddling him, I punched him in the face. Again. And again. And again. Over and over. I would punch him 30,000 times. One punch for every dollar he took away from my future. Every dollar he took away from my new life—a life with Greer.

Jesse was long gone, his face a bloody pulp, before one of the neighbor boys got brave enough to try to knock me off him. Two more held my arms behind my back while we waited for the cops and ambulance to arrive. I felt strangely calm for someone who had just murdered his father with his fists. There was no future for me now, except inside a cell, but I accepted it. My only regret was that I'd tainted my girl's birthday with my crime. It was only a matter of time until she found out.

My college plans, my future with Greer, my dreams for a better life—they'd vanished the moment I'd discovered the missing money. And if I couldn't have them, I didn't want any sort of life at all.

20
GREER

Days passed before I realized what'd happened.
Then weeks.

Jace had beaten his father to death. At first, no one told me anything. We'd spent the rest of my birthday afternoon wandering the wooden piers along Astoria's waterfront, giant cones in hand. Jace had made a show of taking comically large bites of my pink peppermint ice cream while I was distracted watching an amorphous pile of sea lions barking up a storm on a distant pier. When I'd turned back and pretended to be mad, he'd offered me his cone—vanilla—and I put on a show of my own. Jace groaned, taking it back and then kissing me gently on the mouth. Intoxicated by the contrast of cold lips and hot tongue, the bark of the lions and ringing bells of the busy working waterfront, and the cold, spring air buffeting us from all sides, it was the best birthday I'd ever had. A sign of things to come.

Jace hadn't shown up for work the next day, but three days passed before I was worried enough to swallow my pride and ask Sterling. At first, I'd been afraid Sterling had fired him. Then I was afraid something terrible had happened to him, and it had.

Sterling already knew all about it, of course. He had connections all over the city, including within the police department, and everyone knew Jace worked for him. He just hadn't bothered to tell me, punishing me, I'm sure, for entering into a relationship with his employee.

When Sterling finally told me what had happened, I'd tried to visit Jace at the jail facility downtown, but I wasn't on the approved visitor list. I understood. I wasn't upset. Either he was so ashamed of what he'd done, how he'd impacted our future, that he couldn't face me, or he didn't want me to see him locked up. Maybe it was a bit of both.

I'd begged Sterling to go instead, to pull every string he could to get him out and ensure him a fair deal. Knowing Jace, he would take full responsibility for what had happened, but there were mitigating circumstances. There had to be. It was impossible to reconcile the brutality of the act with the man I remembered from my birthday. The one who'd held the door for me as I'd entered the tattoo shop. The stillness of his body as the needle pierced his skin again and again. The apprehension in his eyes as he'd watched me realize the significance of his new tattoo, as if he'd expected me to blow off his gesture. The way he'd devoured his ice cream cone, reminding me of the way he'd devoured me that morning and how he'd teased me for my ever-present blush. The tenderness he'd shown me when he dropped me off, kissing me deeply, possessively, and telling me my birthday was the first of many with him.

I wish he could've stayed longer that night. Maybe this would've never happened. Sterling was gone, and we could've spent the night together, but he'd left. And beaten an old man to death. His father.

His father. Jesse.

Jace was still in jail when I'd recorded and submitted our presentation on the *Jonathan Richmond* in June. In the end, I'd decided not to include any mention of the slave trade. I had no definitive proof, and I couldn't handle the controversy it might set off—at the university or here in town. Oren was right; Sterling had enemies. And the last thing I needed was to alienate Jace's only chance at freedom.

My restraint paid off the day my relentless hounding of Sterling led to the news that the DA had reduced Jace's charges, and he'd soon be released. I couldn't wait to go to him, but I didn't know where he lived. His address wasn't in the phone book, only his phone number, which I called again and again, but no one ever answered.

The future I'd constructed for Jace and myself after our few short weeks together, a future that had been so blindingly bright, was on pause. Regardless, I needed to leave Richmond House. My time had run out. Sterling hadn't come out and said it, of course, but the feeling was instinctual. It was in the air like menace turned visceral, and I took in Sterling's growing impatience with every breath. If Jace wanted to stay in Astoria, we could live in his trailer and go to a local college. I didn't care as long as we were together.

A week before Jace's scheduled release date, I sat on the front porch trying to come up with a plan.

"Greer." Sterling came around from the back of the house dressed in a suit and wool camel coat, his nod to a season that'd never reached its full potential on the warmth front. The bright morning sunlight spotlighted Sterling's old age, his crepe skin and network of wrinkles for once overshadowing his elegantly cut hair and shiny wingtips.

"Sterling," I said, uninterested in anything he had to say.

"Eugenia asked me to speak with you this morning. I

understand this is an awkward time to discuss the topic I'm about to broach, but your...friend...Jace Blackwell will soon be a free man, and from what I understand, you've completed your quarterly academic requirements, so I hope you'll forgive me for inquiring."

"Inquiring what?" I already knew what he was going to say.

"Eugenia and I would like to know how long you're planning to stay at Richmond House."

I should've left weeks ago. But I hadn't. I'd needed to make sure Sterling was committed to helping Jace. Now I didn't know where to go, what to do.

"Not long," I said, wishing for the hundredth time that I could just talk to Jace so we could figure out what to do.

"Are you planning to spend the summer with us? Perhaps play a part in the wedding?"

Gross.

"I don't think so. I plan to leave as soon as I talk...as soon as I can arrange it."

"I understand. Take your time, of course."

Take my time? Yeah, right.

"As I recall, the goal was for you to get to know your mother's family and explore her childhood home," Sterling continued. "I'm sorry we couldn't spend more time together these past few months, but you at least got a taste of our life here in Astoria. I hope you accomplished what you came here to do."

"I sure did," I said, allowing a hint of underlying bitterness to creep into my sugar-sweet tone. "Thank you again for the opportunity to get to know you. I learned quite a bit about you...and my mother."

"But not your father, I gather. Pity."

The silence hung in the air between us before he turned to make his way to the garage. He'd probably been on his way to a business meeting when Eugenia had successfully nagged him into seeking me out. He turned back.

"It's clear that your opinion of me isn't the highest right now," he said, surprising the hell out of me. "At times, I would've said the feeling was mutual, but regardless, you're a Richmond through and through. Sharp. Enterprising. And you clearly do whatever you want regardless of what other people think. And for that reason alone, I'm going to give you a piece of advice. Jace Blackwell has been through a trauma that, God willing, you nor I will ever understand. Just leave the man alone. Whatever it was, it's over between you."

21
JACE

"Blackwell! Visitor!"

The Clatsop County Detention Center in downtown Astoria was small. So small that the visiting room had just three tables. As I made the trip from the cell I shared with two other men, I wondered who'd be sitting there when I walked in. Maybe it was that prick Dave, and he'd offer to give me my money back. But I knew better. That money was already long gone.

I hoped it wasn't Greer, that she hadn't found a way to get to me in here. I'd purposely left her name off my visitor list. As much as I wanted to see her, as much as I wanted to confess to her and beg her forgiveness for the way I ruined what had been the start of something special between us, a bigger part of me didn't want her to see me this way. I'd write to her eventually, and maybe we'd find our way back to each other, but for now, it was over. Gone in an instant, like the money. It was probably for the best.

I turned the corner and saw Sterling sitting at one of the tables, the chair so low the bottom of his camel-colored wool coat was brushing the sticky floor beneath. He'd written to me, requesting to visit, and I'd approved him yesterday. He hadn't wasted any time. Maybe he just wanted to fire me in person—but I held a little of my own ammo to fire back with.

I sat down across from him, but I didn't hang my head. I met his gaze head-on.

"Mr. Blackwell."

"Mr. Richmond."

I wasn't feeling particularly respectful—jail will do that to you, I guess—but Sterling's face had taken on a particular type of evil for me. I'd worked for him for years, and I'm ashamed to say that even if I'd known what I thought I knew now, I still would have. If I hadn't met Greer and fallen for her, it wouldn't have mattered to me the kind of man he was. Greer and I may not have had any proof of his sickness, of his depravity, but I knew in my heart that what we'd uncovered was the truth. And that was before Linus had gotten back to me.

"I was sorry to learn of the circumstances you now find yourself in," Sterling began. "I'm told the charge is second-degree murder. That's quite serious."

"Yeah, well, killing one's father is also 'quite serious.' Don't you agree?"

"It's my understanding that a fit of rage overpowered your ability to reason after you discovered he'd stolen from you. Quite a bit of money."

"Everything I had. But I could reason just fine. I reasoned that I needed to kill him."

Sterling sat back in his chair, steepling his fingers under his chin.

"I find it tasteless to discuss another man's financial situation, especially in a place like this," he said, looking around and finding the visiting room wanting. "But these are special circumstances. I hope you won't be offended if I ask you what you were saving that money for."

I took a deep breath. Normally, I'd tell him to fuck off and mind his own business, but I didn't care anymore.

"The plan was to move out of Navy Heights. Just into an apartment somewhere that was clean and nice. And go to school. Become...something."

"What if I told you that you could still become something?"

"Sure, in twenty years maybe, if they let me out of here."

"What if I told you the District Attorney could reduce the charges against you to manslaughter with cause and your sentence reduced to a fine and community service? Your record would be wiped clean at the completion of your mandated hours."

For killing someone? Even someone as shitty as Jesse?

It didn't seem possible.

"No offense, but I don't have the money to pay any fine. I don't have anything. I'd have to start over, and assuming I still had a job with you, it would take me another few years to even piece together the money for a semester of community college."

"You wouldn't have to attend community college. Upon your release, I would pay your fine and your rent on a furnished apartment here in town or nearby for five years. During those five years, I'd expect you to attend a university of your choosing—I would pay your tuition—and you'd be welcome to continue working in my little shipyard to earn walking-around money. You'd have five years to graduate with a degree and career prospects that would change your life."

I couldn't believe what I was hearing.

"What's the catch?"

Sterling paused as if it pained him to have to say whatever he was about to say out loud.

"We both know that you and my granddaughter are not meant to be. I believe we both want better for her."

Greer. The price I had to pay was Greer. I felt an ache in my chest, right under the tattoo I got to remember her when she eventually left me behind.

"What exactly do you want me to do? I'm sure that as soon as I get out, she's going to come looking for me."

"I suppose. Your job would be to break it off when she does."

"What am I supposed to tell her?"

"Have you pledged your undying love to her? Promised to be with her forever?"

"No, not exactly. But we have...something. We had something. Something special."

"And now you don't. Just tell her you've decided to go in a different direction. Make her understand that this experience has changed you, changed your preferences, so to speak, and you're no longer interested."

I thought about it. I knew deep down I'd already lost her. Even though I knew she deserved the best of everything, and I couldn't give it to her—not yet—there was a time when I'd thought "maybe"...but now there was no chance. Of course, she shouldn't waste her time on me. Of course, she should finish college and build a beautiful life for herself. But the thought of pretending I didn't want her anymore cut deep. I knew what that would do to her.

"No."

"No?"

"I'd rather rot in prison for the rest of my life than manipulate Greer. I won't lie to her. I'll just tell her that we talked today, and the only way you'd help me is if we weren't together anymore."

"I'm afraid that doesn't work for me, Blackwell," Sterling said. "I need Greer to move back to Seattle, away from

Richmond House, and find a man worthy of marrying a Richmond. I need her to settle down and live a quiet life, not continue to stick around Astoria and dig for answers when there are none."

"I'm sorry. I do think Greer's too good for me. Especially now. But I think dumping me should be her choice."

"I didn't want to have to do this, but I think you're forgetting the deal you made with Eugenia. The one where you agreed to take my money in exchange for spending time with Greer and reporting back to us."

I felt sick. It was one thing to dump Greer after everything we'd shared using the "prison changed me" line. It was another for her to find out that our entire relationship had been built on a lie. She'd think I'd never been attracted to her in the first place. She'd think that all the times I'd spoken to her, driven her, held her, kissed her—that it was all for money. That I'd been laughing at her behind her back. She'd wonder how much Sterling paid me to get that tattoo. It would destroy her. She'd struggle with her confidence for the rest of her life. I couldn't let that happen.

"I never did, though. I never told you anything. Greer would understand."

"Would she now?"

"Probably not," I said, huffing out a breath. I was convinced Greer would break up with me all on her own, but I didn't want her questioning the realness of our time together. If it was going to end anyway and I could avoid shattering Greer's entire sense of self-worth *and* twenty years in prison by taking the first step, I'd be stupid not to take Sterling's offer.

I could confront him with what Linus had told me, but I didn't know much. I suspected Sterling's arrest had something to do with Eugenia moving into Richmond House in 1969. Everyone in three counties knew the story—she was fourteen. 'Summer of Love.' I looked down and shook my head in disgust. That would make three victims. Eugenia. Blair. Then Anna. Thank God Blair ran away, or Greer could have easily been next.

I raised my head. How could Greer's eyes be so warm and Sterling's—the exact same color—so cold?

"Okay. Whatever. I'll break it off."

"There's something else I wanted to mention just in case you develop a change of heart and decide to bet on Greer's everlasting love for you rather than her inevitable, lasting feelings of betrayal were she to find out about our previous arrangement. I don't know what fairy tale she spun to get you to believe she sincerely wanted to be with you, but I assure you, she had other plans all along. And it's time for her to go home and act on them."

My heart dropped into my stomach.

"What are you talking about? She invited me to come to Seattle with her. She said she was staying in Astoria with me before...everything happened."

Sterling leaned his head back and laughed.

"Naughty Greer," he said indulgently. "The reason I warned you away from her in the first place is because I learned she already has a boyfriend back in Seattle. He attends the same university. Now that her mother has passed, Greer is free to live with him in his apartment in the U-District, but with you in the picture, she might be tempted to stick around and continue playing the damsel instead of returning to where she belongs."

"No. She would've told me that she was seeing someone."

"I intercepted a letter from him to her, and I have it right here—to Greer Richmond from a Mr. Ryan Johnson of Seattle. Would you like to read it?"

The letter hadn't been opened. I took it from Sterling's

long, spindly fingers, noting the Seattle postmark and return address. The handwriting on the front was masculine. If I tore it open, Greer would know it'd been tampered with. But if I was breaking it off with her anyway, what did it matter?

I took the single sheet of paper out of the envelope. It was dated the night of the dinner party when Eugenia had announced the engagement and Greer had looked so gorgeous in her black dress that my heart ached.

Darling,

Wouldn't you rather correspond via email? I know you said you find letters romantic, but I'm finding them a bit tedious. That said, your last one made me laugh. I can't wait to hear more about your time in Podunk, Oregon. What are you really up to down there, I wonder?

Everything is ready for you here. You mentioned moving a few pieces of furniture from your mother's—let me know as soon as possible which pieces so I can make space. Really, there's nothing you need to bring. Just you.

I love you, Greer Richmond. I can't wait to start our lives together officially.

Yours,

Ryan

I welcomed the anger that surged through my body at the realization of the lies she'd told me. This. This was why I hadn't wanted to go anywhere near Greer Richmond. She showered me with attention, made me feel like we had a future, made me fall in love with her. But it was never real. It was never real. She'd played me.

That bitch!

I folded the letter back up, put it back in the envelope, and handed it back to Sterling. He studied me for a moment.

"I trust that when I say it's imperative you be the one to

break up with Greer and send her back to Seattle as expeditiously as possible—that your release is contingent upon it—we're not going to have a problem."

I nodded. "No problem. Whatever you say."

"Excellent. And Blackwell? I'd really rather you not mention my confiscation of Greer's private mail to her when you two do speak. I wouldn't want her to think I can't be trusted in the future."

22
GREER

Jace returned to Richmond House the last Monday in June, swinging out of the Bronco and heading toward the far edge of the field as if nothing had happened. As if we'd never even met. I'd been watching for him every morning since he'd been released, and when I saw his truck pull up, I could hardly believe it. I forced myself to stop and watch from the window as he got out and walked purposefully through the long grass toward the tool shed at the back of the house. He didn't look up to my window. Didn't knock on the door. Didn't he know I was still here? Did he just not want to talk to me?

He walked from the tool shed to a boat I'd never seen him work on before, all the way on the opposite side of the field from my bedroom window perch. He carried a hose wound into a white five-gallon bucket and a large paint scraper. He set the bucket down near the bow and took a deep breath before he began scraping paint from the side of the wooden boat.

So that's it? You're just going to go to work and not say anything to me?

I raced down the staircase—very Scarlett O'Hara—and

out the back door, stomping my way around the back of the house. I knew he heard me approaching—I wasn't trying to be quiet—but he didn't turn to acknowledge me.

"Jace?" I was afraid the slight tremble in my voice served all my emotions up to him like appetizers on one of Eugenia's gilded trays.

He finally turned around, his lips turned up in a cruel smirk.

"What do you want?"

"You're back."

"Great deduction. It's like you're a detective or something," he said, tapping the handle of the scraper against his nose three times. I searched my mind for something to talk about other than what happened with his dad, his time in jail, our future—he was acting so coldly I couldn't bring myself to dive right in.

"I turned in our research paper. I didn't mention the stuff about the *Jonathan Richmond* carrying slaves or the rumors about the house. Do you think—"

"No offense, Greer, but I'm kind of busy right now. I'm working."

"But...what about..."

"What about what?" He ran his hand through the side of his freshly cut dark hair impatiently.

"What about...us? Our relationship?"

Jace's brows snapped together. He stared me down, angrily. But why?

"We barely had a relationship," he finally answered in a glacial voice that contradicted the fire in his eyes. "We hung out a few times, hooked up a few times. But you know how it is—or maybe you don't. I knew you weren't that experienced, but I thought even you could differentiate between forever love and a fling. Either way, it's not my problem."

He avoided my eyes now, focusing instead on the necklace hanging between my breasts. The pearl shone in the sunshine. He shook his head in disgust, then turned back toward the boat with the scraper, resuming his long strokes. I stood there stunned. Of all the ways I'd imagined our reunion, his cruel rejection of me hadn't been one of them.

"Are you serious right now?" I asked loudly. "That's just…it? We're over?"

He stopped with the scraper and turned back and again stared me down like he hated me. Like he couldn't stand the sight of me.

"Give it up, Greer. There never was a 'we.' Not really. And yeah, I don't want to hook up with you anymore. Sorry to ruin your fun."

A few beats passed. I trembled but resisted the urge to tap. I'd tapped myself ragged since my birthday and look what I had to show for it. If I knew what was good for me, I'd turn and go into the house and never think about Jace Blackwell again. But something wasn't registering. This didn't make any sense.

"What happened? I mean, I know what happened, but what happened at the jail? It's only been, like, two months, and now you're free again. I tried to visit you. I wrote you almost every day. The last time I saw you, you said we were going to spend more birthdays together. 'Many more,' you said. What's changed between then and now?"

"A lot," he answered dispassionately, his frustration obviously building because I wouldn't just accept his explanation and leave.

"I'm sorry, but I don't believe you."

"Believe what you want. Now can I please get back to work?"

"I'm not leaving until I get the real story. I'm not giving up on us."

"Suit yourself. It's your house."

Jace resumed his scraping and not knowing what else to do, I stubbornly sat down in the grass, legs crossed under me, chin in hand. I watched him for hours, tears streaming down my face. He didn't acknowledge me again, never spoke to me once. He went down to his truck around noon and ate a sandwich in the cab, but I stayed where I was. It was like if I let him out of my sight, he'd disappear again.

Late in the afternoon, he collected the supplies he'd been using on the boat and walked them back around the house to the tool shed. Then, he strode past me without a word, back down to the Bronco. He got in, started the engine, and drove away without a backward glance in my direction.

I felt broken but also resolute. I wasn't crazy. What Jace and I had shared might have been brief, but it was intense. It was real. He could act like it was casual, like he'd opened up to every other girl he'd been with the way he had with me, but that couldn't possibly be true. I meant something special to him. And I wasn't backing down until he admitted it.

The next day was more of the same, but this time I was waiting for Jace when he pulled up to the field. Decked out in revealing cutoff shorts and a white tank top, my long hair down around my shoulders, I'd decided looking as sexy as possible could only help me, even if I was cold. And this time, I'd brought a book and one of the chairs from the porch.

Jace wasn't amused.

"Are you seriously going to sit there all day again?"

"Of course not." I tossed my hair over my shoulder. "I might get up and walk around a little. You know, take in the sights."

I wrangled my brows up and down, making it obvious

he was the only sight I was interested in seeing, and I swore I saw his lips ghost into a smile before he shut it down.

"Greer, this is fucked up. I told you I didn't want to be with you anymore, and forcing the issue isn't going to get you what you want."

"I disagree. And like you said, this is my house. I can watch you work if I want to."

The day passed more quickly now that I had a book to distract me. Twice I'd looked up to see Jace watching me. He let our eyes meet before turning back to the boat. Maybe I'd imagined it, but he looked sad. The plan was working—any day now, Jace would tell me the real reason he didn't want me anymore. Or maybe he'd say that everything he'd said when he first got back had been a mistake, and he wanted us to be together again.

On Wednesday, Jace pulled up for work, but he wasn't alone. I watched him from the porch as he slid his big body out of the cab of the truck. The door opened on the other side, and a girl got out. Not a girl—a woman—the opposite of me in every way. She was short with prominent curves, her straight black hair cut off harshly at her shoulders. I couldn't tell what color her eyes were, but I could see from the porch that they were heavily lined. She wore boots and tight jeans, and for a moment, I thought maybe Jace had just recruited her to work alongside him. Until she hooked her arm through his as they walked through the field. She smiled at him, and he looked down as if he only had eyes for her.

It was the first time I'd ever felt jealousy. I didn't count that time in the coffee shop when I'd stared down the barista who'd been looking at Jace like a steaming cup of hotness she'd like to drink up. Jace hadn't even looked at her. But Jace *was* looking at this woman, and it hit me right in the gut. It slowly curled around my insides, wrapping me in a cloak of shame and insecurity.

They walked over to the boat, and I followed behind them, chin up, shoulders back. I took a seat in the chair and crossed my legs like it was a perfectly natural thing to sit and watch a hired man do his work.

She sat up on the deck, her legs dangling down toward Jace as he worked. I couldn't hear what they were saying, but they bantered back and forth for most of the morning, the still morning air occasionally punctuated by their laughter. Jace never looked at me. Not once.

At lunchtime, he jogged back down to the truck. She slid off the boat deck and followed, walking within earshot of me.

"Honey, just leave. This is kind of pathetic, don't you think? He doesn't want to be with you anymore."

I sat frozen. I guess I should thank the generations of Richmonds before me for the absolute ice water in my veins because even though I wanted to scream at her that she didn't know what the *fuck* she was talking about, that I wanted her off my property, even though I wanted to physically beat her to death the way Jace had his father, I did none of those things. I just sat, staring at her coolly until she turned and walked away, shaking her head.

She made her way about halfway down into the field where Jace had unrolled a blanket—the same blanket we'd sat on the day he'd almost run me over. The day he told me about his mom. He'd kept it in the Bronco.

She unpacked a cooler with sandwiches. Jace leaned in and kissed her on the mouth before they started eating. It was a deep, sexual kiss. A lovers' kiss.

I'd like to say that I stayed the course. That I just shook it off. That I was ready to take this woman on and fight for Jace's love. But I didn't. I wasn't. I wasn't strong enough to exist in a space where the person I loved most in the world ignored me. I didn't know how to make Jace want me more than he wanted this new woman. She was right. I was embarrassing myself.

Slowly, so that I didn't attract their attention—or maybe because I knew this was the end and I wanted to prolong the last few seconds I'd ever spend with Jace—I dumped my book and sunglasses into the chair and carried it around the back of the house. I didn't want them to see me take it back up onto the porch—I could do that later. Now, I just wanted to disappear.

Inside, I headed toward Sterling's office door. He'd been spending more and more time away from Richmond House, presumably to avoid his fiancée—who, no doubt, was becoming insufferable to him—or maybe to avoid me, who'd yet to leave, but I knew he was there now because I heard his voice as I approached. The door was cracked open just enough that the conversation happening inside was audible. I stopped myself from peering through the crack to see who was inside. Not that I needed to.

"I did everything you asked, Daddy. When will I get my reward?" Anna's voice was comically, shockingly babyish. I shuddered.

Daddy?

"Soon, darling, though you're looking quite a bit older. Bigger. I'm not sure you deserve your reward."

"I do deserve it. I'm down another few pounds. I'm your baby girl, and I just want to *be* with you again. I ache for you, Daddy."

I turned away in disgust, running down the hall toward the back staircase, and saw Eugenia, who was coming out of the kitchen.

"Greer, darling. Is everything okay? Why are you running?"

"Eugenia, I've decided to return to Seattle as soon as possible. I was wondering if you knew a faster way of booking a flight than driving into town and using the library's Internet to do it."

"I do," she said. "I can call the travel agent right now. When would you like to leave?"

"As soon as possible. Today. Tomorrow. Any time is fine as long as you can also arrange a cab to get me to the airport in time."

She studied me.

"Did you...see something you shouldn't have, Greer?" she asked. I shook my head. "Hear something, then?"

My time here was short. If it worked out, I'd be leaving no later than tomorrow. I might as well get at least what answers I could. I took a deep breath.

"I heard Anna call Sterling 'Daddy.' Is Sterling Anna's father?"

Eugenia's smiling face remained fixed, as if she'd anticipated the question.

"Of course he is, darling. I'd have thought that was obvious by now. It's all very hush-hush, of course. Even now, your grandfather has no interest in 'claiming' Anna as his child—you're still in line to inherit everything. At least until we wed...then Anna will get what's rightfully hers."

"I don't want anything from him. What I heard...Anna made it sound like the two of them had some sort of...relationship."

The indulgent "between-us-girls" look she gave me chilled me to the bone.

"Darling, some men have certain...predilections. Your grandfather has always enjoyed a 'special bond' with the children in his care. A lot of powerful men do. I would stay out of it if I were you. Anna is an adult now, after all, and there's nothing to be done about the various ways in which girls have expressed their love to your grandfather in the past."

I sucked a breath of air into my lungs, feeling like I was going to vomit all over her white apron. What kind of woman was okay with this? What kind of woman wanted to marry a pedophile? Why hadn't she protected her child?

"But she's his daughter. That's...incest." I whispered the last word.

Now, Eugenia's expression was anything but indulgent.

"I think you misunderstood what I was saying," she continued, as if she hadn't just so much as admitted that her fiancé, my grandfather, was a pedophile who'd preyed on my mother, Anna, and who knows how many other girls "in his care." "You're obviously tired—maybe you should go and lie down. I'll make all the arrangements for your departure. I hope you're able to move on with your life and finally let things be. You know...Richmond House has stood for more than a hundred fifty years. With that kind of legacy, there are bound to be casualties. Just be glad you weren't one of them."

I just nodded my head, too distraught to make sense of whatever she was talking about. Carefully avoiding Sterling's office, I made my way up the main staircase, stopping on every third stair, tapping my toe three times before continuing. I couldn't stop, but it didn't matter. I still didn't know who my father was, but I didn't care anymore. I couldn't focus on anything right now except running away.

In my bedroom, I pulled the blackout shades closed without looking back out over the field. I had no more interest in anything Jace Blackwell did. I repeated it in my head twice more. If I said it enough times, maybe it would come true. As I pulled the shade down over my desk, my eyes fell on the fall quarter course catalog I'd neatly filed away in one of the rolltop's built-in cubbies. A sense of relief washed over me when I thought of Eugenia downstairs making the arrangements for me to fly back to Seattle as soon as possible. School didn't start until August, but there was no point in waiting. I knew where I wanted to go. Anywhere but here. And anywhere but home.

Thank you so much for reading *Richmond House*. The story continues in *Richmond's Fall*.

Author Note

The story you just read is fictional, save for a few important details. Astoria is, in fact, a gritty and eclectic port city on the northwest tip of Oregon, home to the Captain George Flavel House, the inspiration for Richmond House. While the story of the city's founding is accurate, most of the locations referenced in the book are imaginary.

The shipwreck of the *Jonathan Richmond* was inspired by the wreckage of the *Peter Iredale*, a four-masted steel sailing vessel that ran ashore Oct. 25, 1906, on the Oregon coast en route to the Columbia River. She was abandoned on Clatsop Spit near Fort Stevens in Warrenton, about four miles south of the Columbia River channel, and her wreckage is still visible on the beach today.

Regarding slavery in the Pacific Northwest: although historians agree that many slaves were brought to Oregon in the mid-1800s, there's no evidence I can find that slave ships docked in Astoria or any other West Coast city.

Also by Leigh Maynard

Richmond's Fall: Astoria Trilogy #2

Coming 4.25.2022

Richmond's Legacy: Astoria Trilogy #3

Coming 6.20.2022

Acknowledgments

I doubt I'd have finished this book if not for the support of my husband, who had never picked up a romance novel in his life, but became my very first reader. He enthusiastically read each chapter as I wrote it, and his feedback made me feel like writing fiction was something I might actually be good at. I'd also like to thank my daughters—who are old enough now to understand what I'm trying to accomplish—for their endless questions about my work. Your understanding and enthusiasm helped keep me going when times got tough.

To my beta readers, Evie-Owen Evert, Jessica Minyard, J.D. Rogers, and Kimberly Skye: I'm so glad I "met" you ladies when I did. Thank you so much for your sharp, scarily astute read-throughs and for teaching me to trust in the process.

I can't thank my editors, Happily Editing Anns, enough for the gentle way they took my story from good to great via their beautiful editing. They are, in large part, the reason you enjoyed this book so much.

Thanks to Sarah Kil Creative Studio for the gorgeous book covers you see throughout this series.

Finally, a word to my parents, bonus parent, sisters, and friends: not everyone feels like their community has their backs, but I'm one of the lucky ones who knows that no matter what I choose to do in life, mine will always support me.

LM

About the Author

Leigh Maynard writes gothic romance from her homes in Seattle, Washington, and Charleston, South Carolina. She lives with her husband, two daughters, and her cat, Henry. When she's not writing, she's reading, skiing, trying to convince her husband she's "outdoorsy," and planning vacations to warmer climes.

Made in the USA
Columbia, SC
13 March 2022